BANDITS, BROADS & DIRTY DAWGS

The Silver Spurs Series: Book Two

by

Laura Hesse

Running L Productions   Vancouver Island, B.C.

Bandits, Broads & Dirty Dawgs /by Laura Hesse

ISBN (print book): 978-1999077471

Cover Design by: AutumnSky, Selfpubbookcovers.com

Distributed Worldwide on Amazon

Publisher: Running L Productions, Vancouver Island, British Columbia Canada.

Publisher Website: www.runninglproductions.com

Acknowledgements

Thank you to all my readers who requested a sequel to *The Silver Spurs Home for Aging Cowgirls* and a big thank you to my Facebook friends who helped me choose a name for this book. You guys rock!

A special thanks to my friend, Dee Gallant, the 'Cougar Whisperer' from Vancouver Island who agreed to appear as a character in this story as well.

For those who haven't read the first book, the Saint Bernard and the paint stallion in this story are based on my buddies, Bulldozer and Add a Patch. May we meet again.

A special thank you goes out to Deb Nicol for being my sounding board for this crazy ride.

Note to Readers

I deliberately took a few liberties with the federal penal system rules and regulations as well as the border crossings between Mexico and the USA in this story.

This is fiction after all!

Bandits, Broads & Dirty Dawgs is a cozy style of western drama-comedy for adult readers who don't mind a little naughty and politically incorrect in their reading list. It will not be for everyone.

On another note, a donkey and a burro are the same thing. When the ladies are south of the border, I tend to use the Spanish name for donkey – burro.

Contents

BANDITS, BROADS & DIRTY DAWGS

The Silver Spurs Series: Book Two

Prelude
The Beginning

If I'm feeling sexy, I'll put on some heels – if that makes me a little taller than you, so be it. You have to be secure enough to stand next to a stallion.
Keri Hilson

Zoe Puddicombe raced along the highway in her little black convertible BMW heading to the penitentiary some seventy-five miles from *The Silver Spurs Home for Aging Cowgirls* where she now resided with her Andalusian stallion, Zippo, and her filly, Extravaganza. The multi-divorcee and widow didn't mind living with the Montana family. Sam Montana was a stud; unfortunately, he was still in love with his deceased wife and possibly the sultry redhead named Sylvie O'Hara. He thought his starry love struck gaze had gone unnoticed, but it hadn't.

Zoe had to confess she liked the brazen outspoken woman. She hadn't meant to have a one night stand with her husband. She had thought Sylvie was an invalid at the time and it wouldn't matter. Zoe had been wrong on both accounts.

Cade O'Hara was a rascal. He brought his mistress with him from Virginia. It was a toss up as to who killed Cade, Maggie or Sylvie, even though Sylvie confessed to his murder.

Zoe wasn't one to hold a grudge and wished Sylvie the best of luck with Sam. At their age, there weren't many single men to choose from and Sam Montana was a catch; although, since the body of Cade O'Hara had never been found, technically Sylvie was still married.

Zoe glanced in the rear view mirror.

"Damn you," she swore as she saw the white dually pass the family in the minivan behind her.

Behind the wheel of the big truck was her nemesis, Maggie Carroll, her cocoa skin and mass of raven hair a stark contrast to Zoe's pale skin and short white spikes tipped with blue. The blue was almost aquamarine. It accentuated her peacock feather earrings and long aristocratic neck.

"You are not going to get there first," she seethed, her brown eyes flashing with anger.

Zoe stepped on the pedal. The beamer shot forward.

Behind her, Maggie followed suit. The big diesel engine bucked, the truck built for towing, not racing with a finely tuned sports car.

Zoe smiled crookedly as she saw Maggie grit her teeth and pound her hands in frustration on the steering wheel as Zoe steadily increased the distance between them.

In truth, they weren't enemies, these two senior women, they were competitors.

Eight months ago, the pair had made a deal: whoever got to the prison first, got to see Tommy first. A game of rock, paper, scissors, decided who got conjugal rights when it was allowed. It wasn't that Tommy was a dream come true or even that he was particularly handsome, in fact, he was rather ugly, but a woman has needs, whatever their age, and Tommy fulfilled both Zoe's and Maggie's without the ladies having to make a lifelong commitment. It suited all concerned or so they thought.

They had met Tommy Cortez after his plane crashed in the mountains close to the Montana ranch. A huge manhunt had ensued. Tommy was a wanted felon – drug trafficking, kidnapping, murder. He had retired but that didn't matter to the law. Justice had been swift. The ladies pounced on the opportunity.

The sheriff's brown and white Suburban passed by going in the opposite direction.

"Damn it," Zoe swore, glancing in the rear view mirror as the sheriff came to a screeching halt and spun the SUV around, red and white lights flashing.

Behind her, the minivan with the family of five in it pulled over to let the sheriff pass as did the one ton dually.

"Darn. Darn. Darn. Darn," the seventy-two year-old woman fumed.

Zoe pulled over to the side of the road, the sheriff pulling his vehicle in behind her. She rolled down the window and waited for her just desserts.

She could argue the ticket and turn on the charm, but that would take time. If she burned rubber, she still might be able to beat Maggie to the prison. The best recourse was to plead guilty and be done with it. What was the worst that could happen? Her insurance would go up and she'd lose some points on her driver's license? She had dressed up for nothing?

Decisions, decisions, she groaned inwardly.

"Mrs Puddicombe, you got a fire to put out," Sheriff Cole Trane drawled as he leaned in the window.

Maggie drove by slowly, a cat that ate the cream grin on her face. She waved regally and pulled away.

"I hate that woman," Zoe spat. "She's never going to let me live this down."

"What woman," the clean shaven good natured sheriff asked.

"Maggie," Zoe simmered.

"Ah, you ladies are off to see Cortez again," Cole grinned, noticing the white dually accelerating on the highway. "What's the appeal? Bad boys and ugly dudes simply turn you on?"

"Oh, Cole," Zoe sighed heavily, rolling her eyes in exasperation. "You wouldn't understand. You're a handsome young man with a pretty sweetheart and your whole life ahead of you. Once you get to my age you realize that all men are ugly so you may as well choose one that adds a little spice to your trysts."

Cole roared with laughter, his grey eyes twinkling.

Cole reminded Zoe of Luke Skywalker. He was handsome in that All American quarterback's way.

"I have to give you a ticket, Mrs. Puddicombe," he said, writing her up. "Next time, either leave a little earlier, lock Miss Carroll in her room, or better yet, find someone else

5

better suited for a spicy tryst. I suggest you come to the next barn dance, I can think of a few fellas there who would be happy to accommodate you."

Zoe snorted in disdain as she plucked the ticket from Cole's outstretched hand. As if she'd be interested in broke down old cowboy?

"See you Sunday," the sheriff grinned as he walked away.

Zoe grinned and waggled her fingers at the sheriff.

It was annoying having the law to dinner every Sunday, but then the sheriff was dating Emma Montana so there was nothing she could do about it. Still, she supposed, he was a nice young man.

Zoe pulled sedately back onto the highway. She was about to step on the accelerator when she noticed Cole following her in the Suburban.

"Seniors, we don't get any respect anymore," she grumbled, her eyes narrowing, her foot itching to put the pedal to the floor.

Chapter One

After the hunt, Lady Thornicroft was asked why her horse was so hot and sweated up? She answered: "If I had you between my legs for two and a half hours dear sir you would be equally as hot and sweaty."

The tall and elegant woman who stepped out of the white pickup truck in front of the maximum security prison stopped to fluff her long mane of silken hair, and check her makeup in the truck's elongated side mirror. She replenished her candy apple red lipstick and smacked her lips together before strutting across the pavement to the entrance. Her preparations for her visit caused the guards to smile. Even though she was old enough to be their mother or grandmother, Maggie Carroll knew how to make an entrance.

"You win today, Miss Carroll," one middle aged guard asked.

"I did," she purred, scratching the smattering of whiskers under his chin with a cherry red fingernail. "You need to shave, Charlie, you're far too handsome to cover up that face."

"Yes, ma'am," the guard blushed as he handed her the sign in sheet.

"I'll let Tommy know you're here," a younger guard stammered as he pressed the radio receiver on his shoulder and notified the guard in the yard.

"I hope when I get to Tommy's age, I can find a woman who looks like that," the middle aged guard murmured as Maggie was buzzed through the first of many security doors.

Maggie's lips twitched into a sly smile as she click-clicked her way across the linoleum floors to the visiting area.

Maggie sashayed into the room, luck giving wings to her step and brightening her usually dour countenance. Forty years as mistress to her best friend's husband had taught her to adapt.

A strange young man in his early twenties with a poorly bleached Mohawk hair cut brushed by her as she sat down in a cubicle to await Tommy's arrival. The boy was wiry and jittery like he had just popped a hit of acid. Maggie turned her back on him, not wanting to garner any unwanted attention from this strange boy-man.

The inmate the boy had visited stood up and was escorted out the door by the guard on the opposite side of the Plexiglas. The inmate was grey haired, paunch bellied and stoop shouldered. He said something funny to the guard on his way out. The guard laughed as he let the inmate out and Tommy in.

Maggie beamed when she saw Tommy's lined face break into a wide grin. The retired drug lord and smuggler was an ugly man, but confidence, animal magnetism, and charisma made up for it, so much so that even the red coveralls he wore couldn't dampen it. In fact, the broad shouldered bandy-legged prisoner looked rather yummy.

"Maggie, my love," he grinned, lifting the phone and speaking into the receiver.

Prison life suited her beau. He was more relaxed and a whole lot chubbier than when she had first met him; although, he had been dehydrated and suffering from heat stroke and hunger after three weeks of being stranded in the mountains with a broken leg.

"Hello, sweetheart," Maggie grinned. "Don't you look delicious?"

Tommy laughed.

"That's why I love you, dear," he chuckled. "You lie so well, but I did get my hair cut yesterday."

"Ooooh, let's not use that 'L' word, you know how I feel about that," Maggie muttered.

"Why does it frighten you so much," he asked, his dark brown eyes glinting, his brow furrowing.

Maggie shrugged. In truth, she couldn't answer that question if she wanted to, because she didn't know herself. Tommy wasn't the type to be trifled with so no answer was better than a lie.

"And here I thought you wanted to be my pirate queen and sail off on the high seas with me. It's not too late you know, I could arrange it," he whispered fiercely.

"Pirate queen, yes, but only if I'm the one standing on the bridge with a cutlass in one hand and a pistol in the other," Maggie chuckled, thinking he was kidding. "You know me, Tommy, I have to be charge."

He was kidding, right?

"What's got into you today?"

"Nothing," Tommy said, leaning back in his chair. "I was just wondering if you really cared for me or if I was just someone to pass the time with, someone you think you can twirl around your pinkie, brag about at the hair dresser."

"Oh, please, we've discussed this before," she replied smugly.

What did he expect? Did he think that she would run away with him on a whim, or that it was possible to escape from this maximum security Hell hole? Not likely!

"Have they told you when we can have our next in-person visit," Maggie purred, drumming a manicured nail on the counter. Tommy hadn't been the only one to spruce up for visiting day.

"Not until next month, I'm afraid," he pouted, his craggy face seeming to crumble before her eyes. The expression made him look ghoulish. "I guess you're just going to have to wait for your next cleaning."

"Don't be so vulgar," Maggie exploded, hanging up the phone. She wouldn't be talked to like this, not by some drug lord has been.

Tommy's eyes glittered menacingly, his wide jaw set resolutely in a mock offended mask. The look he gave her made Maggie shiver. She should have let Zoe see him first.

Maybe he would have been in a better mood after seeing that dip stick.

She waited for him to indicate that she should pick up the phone again so he could apologize, but it never happened. He was in a mood!

Anger simmered just below the surface. Two could play at that game. Maggie smirked, tossed her hair back, and stormed out of the cubicle. She banged on the door for the guard to let her out. It probably wasn't the smartest of moves. Tommy still had men on the outside. At the moment, she was so irate, she didn't care.

A pirate queen – not likely!

"Done already, Miss Carroll," the guard asked politely.

"Oh, I'm done all right," she growled as she stalked away. "You can let Zoe in now if she's here."

***

The guard in the visitor's area looked askance at Tommy through the Plexiglas. Tommy raised both hands in supplication. The two men shared a laugh.

Zoe glided into the room in a loose silk blouse, peacock earrings, black jeans and leather riding boots. She wasn't as elegant as Maggie, or as tumultuous, but Tommy loved her as much as the raven haired beauty that made his legs go weak and his heart go pitter-pat.

Zoe was pretty in her own way, not as beautiful as Maggie, but lovely all the same. She was open and earnest without a nasty bone in her body. He knew the ladies liked to compete for his affections, and he had been enamoured by the pair. Who wouldn't be? He was seventy years old and had two classy dames fighting over him? Mrs. Puddicombe was easy to please. She reminded him a lot of his lovely Louisa.

Tommy crossed himself at the thought of his deceased wife. Zoe settled herself in the booth across from him and lifted the telephone receiver.

"I'm so glad you made it," Tommy said, his spirits lifting as he gazed into Zoe's brown eyes.

"Me too," the widow tittered. "I don't know what you said, but you sure got under Maggie's skin."

"Maggie's always angry," Tommy laughed.

"She is that," Zoe agreed.

"You, my lovely Zoe, have washed away the rain and brought the sun back into my life with your very presence," the inmate grinned.

"Now that's a bit much," Zoe replied delightedly, her feathered earrings bouncing sensually against her neck.

"Maybe, but it's true," Tommy marvelled, leaning forward. "I miss you when you don't come. You weren't here last week. I don't care about the conjugal visits, I enjoy your company. You are always so happy."

"Oh, that's so sweet," Zoe blushed.

Tommy was pleased that Zoe was here, but disappointed in Maggie's fiery reaction to his offer to be more than just his girlfriend. Perhaps he should have been more direct? He really thought she would be happy with his casual mention of the 'L' word. The smuggler had more money than the Pope. He could arrange a jail break. He almost laughed at the spectacular headlines that would have caused.

"Are you okay, honey, you look terribly sad all of a sudden," his second lady asked him.

"I was thinking about how much better it would be to have a wife visit me rather than two pretty senioritas," he said, tossing it out there.

Zoe's big eyes got even rounder.

"What," she stammered. "What do you mean?"

"Isn't it obvious? I want to marry you, Mrs. Puddicombe," the grizzled old man replied silkily, casting the chair aside, and getting down none to gracefully on one knee.

"Are you serious," she gasped, her mouth falling open to reveal a perfect set of white teeth.

She should be in a toothpaste commercial, Tommy mused.

"I am."

"But, but...," she stuttered.

"But I am in prison for life," he said sadly, still on one knee. "I am not a monster, but I am capable of being one. I am tired. I am old. I want a woman to weep for me when I die. You would be well taken care of. So, Zoe Puddicombe, will you or will you not marry me?"

"I don't need your money, Tommy," the shell shocked woman sighed. "I have more than enough."

"And?"

"Oh, what the heck, Zoe Cortez has a nice ring to it," Zoe cried, placing a hand on the glass.

"Hear that, guys, she said 'yes'," Tommy barked, casting aside all thoughts of the fierce raven haired woman who had stormed out on him earlier. His heart swelled with happiness as the lone guard behind him clapped him on the back.

"Help me up, will you, amigo," he asked the guard.

Zoe clasped a hand over her mouth, tears welling in her eyes.

"Don't cry, baby," Tommy urged her. "I'm going to call my youngest son, JJ. You're going to love him and he's going to love you. I'm going to have him buy you the biggest diamond you've ever seen. Elizabeth Taylor will be turning in her grave."

Zoe laughed, kissed one finger and placed it against the glass. Tommy grinned and placed a finger over hers.

"Sorry lovebirds, but your time is up," the guard said. "Congrats though."

"Okay, okay," Tommy grimaced.

Zoe went to hang up the intercom phone, but Tommy pointed at the ear piece. There was one last thing he wanted to tell her before she hung up, maybe advise her not to discuss their engagement with Maggie lest his fiancée wind up in an unmarked grave somewhere like Maggie's long time lover.

Maggie had told him about Cade's demise after a particularly passionate love making session. That woman had a temper. Unfortunately, the guard on the other side of the glass plucked the phone out of Zoe's hand and hung it up for her. Tommy was going to have to have a few words with him. Money talked and so did influence.

14

"I love you," he mouthed to her as he was escorted away.

"Love you too," Zoe mouthed as she was whisked out of the visitor's room by the guard.

Tommy couldn't hide the grin on his face as he walked down the hall. The stink of disinfectant and humanity assailed his senses. In reality, he didn't mind it. He could have been placed in a much worse of a place.

"What's got you all hot and bothered," his cellmate, Bruce Park, asked as Tommy entered the cell. "Oh, wait, let me guess, you organized another conjugal with one of those hot broads of yours. You know, those dames are pretty tasty for their age."

"Hey, cabrón, mind your manners, I'm gonna marry one of them," Tommy grinned.

"Congrats man," the grey haired fat man replied, shaking Tommy's hand, a false grin on his face.

Tommy let it pass. Nothing was going to ruin the rest of his day.

Chapter Two

Just because a talking donkey tells you something doesn't mean it's true.
Matt Mikalatos

Sam Montana swung the post hole digger attachment arm to one side and turned off the John Deere tractor. The slim silver haired white moustached Marlboro Man of a cowboy climbed off the tractor and went to help his grandson finish the job.

BJ muscled the last wood post into the hole. It landed with a hollow thump.

It always amazed Sam how much his grandson looked like his father, Cleve. BJ was only eight when his father died. Now, he was fifteen and shaping up to be a fine young man with his curly mop of black hair and sky blue eyes. He wasn't afraid of hard work either.

"I'll square her up while you fill 'er in," Sam drawled, wiping the sweat from his brow with his pocket handkerchief. "For a spring day, it sure is a hot one."

"I heard a few men talking at the feed store last week. They said the Farmer's Almanac is predicting a scorcher," BJ agreed.

Usually at this time of year there was still snow in the fields, not just in the foothills and on the mountain top.

"I was thinking the same thing," Sam nodded. "Next week, we'll finish branding the cattle. I figured we'll be pasturing them up in the high country this summer. I'm glad we only bought fifty head to start with. We'll see how the year shapes up."

"You worried about rustlers," his grandson asked.

"Rustlers in this day and age," Sylvie asked as she, Mary, and Emma brought sandwiches and a cooler full of iced tea and Pepsi cola out to the men.

"Rustlers are a huge problem everywhere and not just cattle either," Mary informed Sylvie. "Even Florida wasn't immune. I was terrified that one day, I'd wake up to find my Patches gone."

"Well, I'll be horn swaggled," Sylvie replied, slapping her knee.

"Horn swaggled, is it," Sam grinned, his hazel eyes sparkling.

"Maybe I should hitch up my jeans, load up my six guns, and ride the range," the red-headed spitfire offered, narrowing her eyes and imitating twirling a moustache.

Mary and Emma exploded into a raucous round of laughter.

"And just who are you going to ride out on the range on," Mary stammered, handing BJ and Sam a roast beef sandwich. "That stallion of yours isn't built for cutting

17

cows. He's so tall you couldn't even bend down to pat one."

Mary's silver blond hair sparkled in the sunshine. Many a man took the eighty-year-olds diminutive frame as a sign of frailty, but she was anything but weak.

Sylvie on the other hand was a cracker, as his father would have said. Sam wasn't surprised when they named a hurricane after her this year.

"Who said I was planning on riding the range on a horse," Sylvie winked conspiratorially at Sam.

"Cover your ears, BJ," Sam told his blushing grandson.

"Oh, shucks, BJ is a young man now," Sylvie remarked, "he's long since learned about the birds and the bees."

"The birds and the bees are one thing, you're something else," Emma moaned, wagging a warning finger at the former hunt seat rider.

"Well, in another hour or so, we'll have the stallion pens finished," Sam mumbled between bites of sandwich.

"The pens look great," Emma said, casting a look over the five long sections of fenced off pasture.

"Buddy's never been out on pasture like this," Sylvie added, taking in the green expanse. "He'll think he's died and gone to Heaven."

"Patch has. He's going to love having open space again," Mary smiled.

"You think that crazy Andalusian and Trakehner stallion will take to it," Sam wondered. "I'm pretty sure Zippo will, but I'm worried Desert Storm will jump into one of the other pastures. I've wired up the electric fence, but I'm not sure that's enough."

"Who are you thinking of putting where," Sylvie asked, her brow furrowing.

"I'm gonna put Extravaganza in the first pasture since she's due to foal in three months or so, and I thought I'd put Zippo beside her because they are so bonded," Sam pointed at the pasture closest to the back of the barn where Mary's stallion and the one eared donkey named Mike hung out. "When she's close to her time, she can go in Patch and Mike's pen."

"That's a good idea," Mary agreed.

"After that will be Patch and Mike, and then Buddy and Desert Storm in the last two pastures."

The ladies all nodded.

"Speaking of Patch and Mike, where's Jenny," Sam asked his daughter-in-law. "I thought she'd be out here riding her pony or fussing over Mike."

"She's in the house doing research on the computer," Emma smirked. "I'm not exactly sure what kind of research."

"That can't be good," Sam guffawed.

"I know, but she wants to surprise you," BJ said to his mum. "Don't worry, it ain't nothing bad."

"Oh, dear, I'm not sure I'm ready for this," Emma groaned.

"We thought we might introduce Boomer and Bucky to Buddy, Mrs Cade," BJ ventured, changing the subject.

Sam knew instantly that his grandson was hiding something. He agreed with Emma. Surprises and Jenny weren't a good mix.

"Since Boomer's not ridable anymore and Bucky is my cow horse, we thought it would be good for Buddy to have company and it might settle down Mrs Carroll's stud having another horse on the other side of the fence in case we pull Bucky and Buddy out at the same time," BJ said, rubbing the mustard on his fingers onto his jeans. The jeans were so stained with grass and dirt, the mustard blended right in.

"That leaves us with the three mares, Penny, Checkers and Rosie," Sam noted. "I figured we'd leave the mares in the cow pasture."

"That all makes sense to me," Sylvie agreed.

"I think so too," Mary responded.

"It depends on princess throwing a wrench in the works by having to walk too far to retrieve her stallion," Sylvie said.

"Yeah, that is the one tool in the shed that needs sorting out," Sam nodded, pushing his Stetson back on his head.

"Speaking of Maggie, here she comes now," Emma noted, nodding towards the white dually truck speeding up the lane.

"Damnable woman, what does she think she's doing driving into the ranch like that," Sam growled, pushing past the women. He strode purposefully towards the woman driving carelessly into the yard.

"Oh, oh," Emma stammered, dashing after her father-in-law.

"I love a good argument, don't you," Sylvie said, wrapping her arm under Mary's.

"BJ, you better stay here," Mary called over her shoulder. "It might be safer."

"No argument there, ma'am," BJ agreed, opening the drink cooler. He plucked a can of ice cold Pepsi out of the blue cooler, popped the tab, closed the cooler's lid, and sat down on the ground to watch the fireworks.

Sam vaguely heard the conversation behind him. He knew he was acting like a bull charging a matador, but couldn't help himself.

What if his granddaughter rushed out of the house? She was precocious and always on the move. Jenny wouldn't expect to see a truck speeding into the yard.

"Slow down, Maggie," Sam hollered, holding one hand up in the air in a 'halt' position.

Maggie slammed on the brakes, threw the gears into park, and stepped out of the truck, her face pinched, her mouth a thin line.

"What's your problem," she glowered.

"Don't you ever drive into the yard like that again," Sam warned her, his temperature hitting the boiling point.

"Fine," she snipped.

"Fine," he barked back.

Maggie spun on her high heeled boots, stomped across the yard, and into the house just as Jenny flew out the door, the girl's big grin fading as the rude woman stormed past her.

"What'd I do this time," the curly haired girl wailed.

His Raggedy Anne of a granddaughter raced off the porch and into his arms. Sam's heart melted as he wrapped his arms around her.

"You didn't do anything, sweet pea, Maggie's just in one of her moods again," Sam consoled her.

"Are you sure," she sniffed.

"He's sure, honey," Emma replied, joining in the hug.

"Don't pay any attention to Maggie, Jenny," Sylvie added. "I don't know how many times she's almost run me over, either two-wheeling or four-wheeling," Sylvie said. "She can be a b…"

"Bad tempered woman sometimes," Emma broke in.

"That's a good word for it," Mary piped in cheerily.

"I'll go have a talk with her," Sam grumbled, pulling out of the family hug.

"How about you let me chop that tree down, cowboy," Sylvie offered. "I've had an awful lot more practice than you in this matter."

"Fair enough," Sam agreed, but not without reservations.

"There's a nice cold pitcher of iced tea on the porch," Mary smiled. "It's perfect to cool off with."

"Yes, let's all get out of the sun and you can tell us what this research you've been doing is about," Emma said, casting a look at Sam that spoke volumes. He was going to sit down and have a glass of iced tea whether he wanted to or not. Sam knew better than to argue.

Jenny's face brightened instantly.

"Race you," Mary challenged the child.

Jenny was off in a split second, Maggie Carroll's tantrum a thing of the past. Mary fake jogged across the yard after her, pumping her arms in slow motion as if she was really trying to win.

Sam, Emma and Sylvie walked side-by-side across the rest of the yard. They climbed up the two front steps of the sprawling two-story ranch house. Sam had to admit the pitcher of iced tea sitting on the hand hewn logged table looked pretty good.

"You sure you want to deal with her," Sam asked Sylvie quietly.

"Have I let you down yet," she replied demurely.

"No, ma'am."

"She probably lost to Zoe again," Sylvie snorted derisively. "What the two of them see in that old bandit is beyond me."

"It's beyond any of us," Emma agreed.

Mary poured and Jenny handed out five glasses of iced tea.

Sam sat down in his favourite wood rocker and sipped his drink. It hit the spot. He was hot, tired, and sweaty and ruffled, all in that order.

Sylvie, Mary and Emma sat down in the other weathered straight backed wooden chairs.

"Okay, Jenny-penny, spin your yarn," Sam teased his granddaughter.

Jenny sat cross-legged on the ground in front of her mother and grandfather.

"So, BJ and me found us a poster at school. The school is doing a fundraiser this year," Jenny said excitedly. "One of the teachers did the race in Creede, Colorado. She said she had the time of her life so they're going to do one here next month. All the money raised is going to be split between the school and a local rescue."

"And exactly what kind of race is it," Emma inquired.

"And what rescue society is involved," Mary asked, leaning forward.

"It's a Donkey Rescue," Jenny smiled, her grin stretching from ear to ear.

"What does that have to do with racing," Sam queried, confused.

"It's a donkey race, grandpa," Jenny huffed. "I'm gonna train Mike to run with me."

The three women sitting beside Sam looked as startled as he was.

"I'm gonna need your help with old Mike," the little girl babbled on. "I have to train him to jog alongside me. You see, you don't ride your donkey, it's a partnership. That's what the teacher said. There are vet checks along the way and stops for water."

"I see, and how long is this race," he mumbled, trying not to laugh at the image that popped into his mind: a one eared donkey jogging along beside a carrot topped curly haired girl with a face full of freckles and a head full of dreams.

"It's five to twenty-five miles. You can choose how long you want to race for. Several of the kids from my class are pairing up with donkeys from the rescue. They're only doing the five miles so I figured I'd do that too. BJ said he might join me and do maybe ten or fifteen miles, but I think that's only because Bessie told him she was going to do it."

"Who's Bessie," Emma and Sam asked together.

"Just a girl," Jenny replied guiltily.

24

Sam and Emma exchanged another look. This was news!

"Donkey racing? Who'd have thought?" Sylvie grinned.

"It's the end of days," Mary chuckled. "It must be."

"It's the end of days alright. On that note, I think I'll go upstairs and have a chat with Maggie," Sylvie said, placing her empty glass on the table and slipping quietly into the house with a backwards glance at Sam.

"And I think I'll go give Patch a brush down," Mary grinned.

"Yep, and I'm fixing to have a man to man talk with my grandson while we put in that last post and rail," Sam grumbled as he stood up.

"Can I go with Mary and groom Mike," Jenny bubbled, speaking so fast it was hard to understand her.

"Only if I go with you," Emma agreed. "I want to hear more about this donkey race and exactly what you expect of Mike."

"And you can tell us girls all about this Bessie girl," Mary quipped. "She isn't actually a cow, is she? Let's clear that up lickety-split."

"No, she's not a cow," the nine year-old giggled. "She's really pretty. Bessie's got hair like corn silk, just like yours, Mary, and she's uber-smart."

Sam sighed heavily as he strode back across the yard to where BJ had already started filling in the ground around the last post. He noticed the dogs, two Saint Bernards, Bulldozer and her eight month old pup, Dozer Junior, asleep atop the manure pile.

So much for an uneventful spring, Sam moaned. Two crazy old women with the hots for a jailed felon, four stallions, a pregnant uppity mare, a one eared donkey who was about to become a marathon racer, a married woman that he couldn't touch for fear of eternal damnation, and now a grandson with a girlfriend that the boy wasn't talking about. It looked like it was going to be a long time before peace returned to the Montana family spread.

Still, Sam consoled himself, it could have been much worse: they could have lost the ranch to the bank last year. They would have too if they hadn't turned it into a retirement home for seniors with horses. In less than a year, the ranch was out of debt, the taxes paid, and he had fifty head of cattle mowing down the winter pasture.

Yep, he thought, repositioning the sweat stained Stetson on his head; the serene life on the ranch was over… at least until it became too much for them and they asked the ladies to leave. Given how attached the family had become to them, the likelihood of that happening was non existant.

Chapter Three

A horse doesn't care how much you know until he knows how much you care.
Pat Parelli

Maggie heard Sylvie's soft knock upon her door. She didn't want to answer it, but knew her childhood friend wouldn't quit until she did. Maggie and Sylvie had been friends for sixty years.

"Come in, Sylvie," she called, staying where she was, seated by the window in a Queen Anne's chair, a throw blanket tucked around her lap. A shot glass filled with Irish whiskey sat on the table beside her. The sun streaming through the window made her black hair look almost blue. The few white strands along the temples glittered like a frozen waterfall.

"You don't usually drink in the afternoon," Sylvie said as she opened the door and walked into the room.

"If you want a shot, you'll have to get a glass from the bathroom," Maggie sulked.

Her nerves had been on edge ever since her visit with Tommy. Her anger had slowly receded thanks to the double shot of whiskey she'd already downed, but a gut wrenching agony coiled like a mighty python inside of her.

"Too early for me," Sylvie replied, approaching her friend.

Sylvie sat down on the edge of the bed and looked Maggie in the eye. Maggie tried to speak, but tears fell instead and she snapped her mouth shut.

"Damn it," she croaked, reaching for a Kleenex.

"What happened, Mags," Sylvie whispered after Maggie had dried her eyes.

"He asked me to be his pirate queen and run away with him," Maggie sniffed.

"He did, did he," Sylvie snorted. "And how did he plan on doing that, sprout wings?"

"That's not the point," Maggie retorted, straightening up. "He used the 'L' word."

"He actually confessed his love for you?"

"Well, not directly, but it was implied, and he seemed serious about me running away with him," the distraught woman scowled.

"That's just silly," Sylvie continued. "The man is in a maximum security prison. You can't bribe your way out of there, even if you are some prize bozo off the America's Most Wanted list. Tommy's not that tough."

"Oh, I think he is," Maggie disagreed.

Tommy had let some things slip after their lovemaking that had given her serious pause, but who was she kidding, she was seventy-one years old. She knew she looked good for her age, but the only eligible man around here was Sam and he despised her. Maggie wasn't a ninny. She saw the dislike in Sam's eyes when he regarded her.

"He's not as tough as you, Mags," Sylvie replied, picking up Maggie's hand and holding it tightly.

"I did tell him that the only way I'd run away with him was if I was the one standing on the bridge with a sword in one hand and a pistol in the other," Maggie chuckled.

"See? That's what I mean," Sylvie laughed. "You're a beautiful and strong woman. You always were, even when we were kids. I used to envy you your strength of will. I should have kicked that cheating husband of mine to the curb years ago. You would have."

"But I didn't, Sylvie," Maggie said, the words catching in her throat. "I cheated on you, my best friend, for years. I still don't know why I did. It was mean and it was cruel. I don't know how you've managed to forgive me."

"Because we have memories together, the good along with the bad," Sylvie croaked.

Maggie looked into Sylvie's mesmerizing blue eyes and wondered if her friend truly had forgiven her.

"Look, that old bandit is not worth this upset and you charged in here in my truck like Mario Andretti," Sylvie chastised her. "So, dry your tears and go apologize to Sam Montana and swear you won't do it again. If Jenny or BJ had been in the yard and you hurt them or one of the dogs or anyone else, you'd be gone."

"No, I wouldn't," Maggie chirped, her feathers ruffled. "Sam and Emma need my money, yours too. They'd lose the ranch if we took our horses and departed."

"Who says if Sam kicked you out that I'd go," Sylvie retorted, her expression hardening.

Maggie went cold. A sweeping Artic chill froze the whiskey in her gut.

"What ever do you mean," she scowled. Surely, Sylvie was jesting.

"I'm saying that if you don't start behaving better, don't count on me following you back to Virginia or anywhere else you choose to go," Sylvie glowered. "I like it here. Emma, Sam and the kids have welcomed us into their homes like family and we didn't deserve it. I will do everything in my power to earn and keep their respect now and in the future."

"You're just saying that because you are in love with Sam," Maggie said, waving a hand dismissively in Sylvie's direction. "He'll never marry you. He can't unless Cade's body is found. It's a catch twenty-two, isn't it? If they find the body, you can marry the man of your dreams, but you'll go to jail for murder. You'd be in the same situation as I am only in reverse."

"If you can't see the difference between me and you, then we have nothing left to talk about," Sylvie hissed. "I told Sam that I'd talk some sense into you. The ball's in your court. Do what you will, but live with the consequences. It's high time you did!"

Sylvie stalked out of the room, slamming the door shut behind her.

Maggie was on edge. She had never seen Sylvie so angry. She downed the whiskey, the dark liquid burning her throat, poured another shot, and then downed it too.

The chill in her heart and soul didn't abate. Never had Maggie felt so alone, but then, that was the crux of it, wasn't it? Maggie hadn't slept with Cade to compete with Sylvie. She had slept with Cade because she was so darned lonely.

***

Sylvie's hands shook perceptibly as she exhaled and inhaled, counting each breath, working steadily to calm her nerves as she left Maggie's room and climbed down the stairs. She regretted her harsh words, but Maggie had to learn to turn it off. Sam wouldn't put up with much more and frankly, Maggie's behaviour was getting old.

Maggie had never had a sunny disposition, but Sylvie had never realized how deeply rooted her bitterness was. Bitterness and neediness, she supposed.

Maggie had everything growing up: money, beauty, brains, handsome suitors, but it was never enough.

Perhaps Sylvie had been overly hard on her, but she didn't know what to do. Changes had to be made.

Maggie needed to realize that if Sam kicked her out, Sylvie would not follow her. Sylvie had come to love Emma and the kids and perhaps she was in love with Sam Montana, but neither of them would ever act upon it. Murder was a serious business and she had killed Cade in cold blood. It wasn't premeditated, simply a thoughtless act of revenge caused by a lifetime of broken promises and pain. Sylvie had loved Cade and in her own way missed him dearly. That didn't excuse her actions. She was repentant, but it was too late to do anything about it.

Sylvie changed out of her sneakers and tugged on her battered leather mud boots. Some time with her horse was what she needed. The gentle giant had been her therapy horse for years.

It was early enough to go for a short ride before dinner. Maybe Jenny, Mary or Emma would join her since Zoe wasn't back from the prison yet.

Zoe burst into the house at that exact moment.

Speak of the devil, Sylvie mused.

"Don't you look radiant," Sylvie complemented the woman.

Zoe positively glowed. If Sylvie hadn't known it was simply visiting day, she would have sworn the grinning woman had just had a conjugal visit.

"Thank you," Zoe gushed, "except for the speeding ticket courtesy of our handsome local sheriff, it has been a marvellous day."

"Oh, really," Sylvie grinned, the woman's happiness spreading outwards. "Come on, spill the beans."

"There's nothing to spill," she replied slyly.

"You're hiding something, I can tell."

"Ooooh, you're dressed for riding," Zoe said, looking Sylvie up and down. "Let me get changed and I'll join you."

Sylvie was dumb stuck as Zoe almost galloped up the stairs, flew into her bedroom and closed the door, humming away as if she hadn't a care in the world.

32

"I'll see you in the barn," Sylvie called after the dancing woman.

"Won't be long," the woman called back.

There wasn't a peep from Maggie's room.

Sylvie marched out the door wondering if that rascal, Tommy Cortez, had asked Zoe to be his pirate queen too. She wouldn't put it past him and she wouldn't put it past Zoe to agree.

"Good Lord, I hope she doesn't plan on making Tommy Cortez husband number seven," Sylvie mumbled as she ambled across the yard to the barn, waving to Jenny, Mary and Emma in the far sand paddock.

"Zoe and I are going for a ride, you gals want to come," she shouted.

"That sounds marvellous," Mary called back.

"We're in," Emma yelled, wrapping an arm around her daughter's shoulder.

Jenny gave Sylvie a thumb's up.

Chapter Four

If you are a rider, the number one thing to do is ... marry money!
Anonymous

Benny Park and Percy James sat huddled together in a corner table nursing a couple of Coronas in the half empty bar.

"So my dad says this Tommy Cortez guy is loaded," the brown eyed edgy young man whispered to his buddy seated across the table.

"Yeah, but isn't he connected," Percy whispered back. "Wasn't he former cartel or something?"

"I don't think so," Benny said. "He was just a drug runner and coyote. If he was cartel, I don't think they'd have let him retire alive, if you know what I mean."

"Still, you don't get on America's Most Wanted list by being some low level dude."

"What? You scared of some old geezer? Come on, the guy has to be eighty or something. What's he gonna do, chase after us with his walker?"

"He can't be that feeble if he's got two girlfriends visiting him every week," the blond haired blue eyed twenty-one year-old replied.

"I guess. I trust my dad though. He says the guy is loaded and loves both those broads," wheedled Benny. "All we got to do is nab them and tell him to pay up. A cool million each - how's that for a few days work? Easy-peasy, brother. My old man says he struts around the yard like a peacock. He wants to wipe the grin right off his face."

The two men laughed and clinked glasses.

"So, how we gonna do this," Percy asked.

"The broads don't come at the same time. Pops says they aren't allowed to visit together so if we nab the first one as she's leaving, and then grab the second one when she comes out of the jail afterwards, we can kill two birds with one stone."

"What if they come out together," Percy asked worriedly.

"Bro, you really think we can't handle two crazy broads in their seventies," Benny scowled. "Don't wimp out on me. I need you."

"I'm just saying that there's got to be cameras in the front of the prison and trying to kidnap two old ladies at once out'a the parking lot is going to raise an alarm. I don't want to get shot."

"We aren't gonna get shot and I told you, those old ladies don't arrive together," Benny assured his partner, playfully punching him on the arm. "Pops says Cortez told him the ladies can't stand each other. Ain't that a lark?"

35

"It does sound like an easy job," Percy mumbled.

"Easy money, bro, easy money," Benny grinned, waving to the waitress, and holding two fingers in the air.

"I figure we steal a panel van, grab one broad, tie her up and gag her, and then take off when we got the next one. We'll ditch the van and move them into my Bronco. We'll hide them up in the mountains until pay day."

"We aren't gonna hurt them though, right," Percy stuttered, leaning back as the waitress delivered two more beers.

"I mean, that would be like mugging your grandma," Percy continued after Benny had paid for the drinks and the waitress was out of ear shot.

"Of course not," Benny smiled crookedly, his spiked blond and brown hair seeming to bristle.

"I'm serious, Benny, you got a mean streak sometimes," the younger man mumbled.

"Look, I promise you that so long as they don't cause me no trouble, I won't so much as pluck a hair from their silver heads," Benny agreed.

"All right, let's do it then," Percy beamed, before taking a long swig of beer.

Benny stiffened. Someone was watching him! He turned and saw the bartender staring his way. Benny chugged his beer, flipped the guy the bird, and hauled his scrawny frame out of the bar stool.

"Come on," he ordered Percy. "Let's go look for a place to stash the ladies."

Percy downed his beer, threw a couple of bucks on the table for a tip, and slipped out of his chair.

The bartender and the waitress shared a laugh as they watched the two men leave the bar. They had seen their type before, want-to-be tough guys with spiked hair and attitudes, but not enough brains to pull anything off. The pair had no idea how right and how wrong they were in judging the various degrees of bad.

***

Tommy stood in the hall talking into the one phone on his cell block that the inmates were allowed to use.

"That's right, JJ, I want you to buy me a rock, the biggest one you can get," Tommy grinned into the phone.

"Seriously, pops, did I hear you right? You're getting married," came the surprised reply. "I mean, why?"

"What? You think your old el abuelo is too old to fall in love and get married," he laughed.

"I didn't say that, I'm just surprised, is all."

"Wait until you meet her, JJ, she's beautiful and rich," Tommy gushed. "This woman could have any man she wants, but she loves me."

"She's rich, you say," his son added. "And you're sure she's not after your money?"

Tommy was touched by JJ's concern. He was a good boy. All of Tommy's children had walked away from the life Tommy had carved out for himself. Tommy was proud of them. Edwardo, his oldest, had become a doctor and moved to the US where he married a pretty American, and his daughter had become an accountant. She married an American service man and lived outside of Washington.

37

"Si, she lives on a ranch which caters to seniors with horses," Tommy chuckled. "Can you believe that? My fiancée is a vaquera. Wait until you see her beautiful horses. I know you will love her. I want Zoe to have a big rock, but not too big. My vaquera is diminuta."

"Okay, papa, I'll get you your ring, but promise me you won't get your heart broken by this woman," JJ asked of him.

"She will not break my heart and I swear on your mother's grave that I will not break hers either," Tommy advised the young man.

"Okay, I'll be down in a few days."

"That's good, I'll see you then," Tommy said, hanging up the phone.

The man behind him slapped him on the back.

"Hey, rocking it, gramps," the toothy youngster smirked.

"You touch me again like that, gringo, and I'll slice off your fingers and stuff them down your throat," Tommy whispered into the younger man's ear, a false smile spreading across his craggy face as he slammed a shoulder into the inmate with bull dog force.

The kid staggered back and put his hands up in the air in supplication as Tommy swaggered back to the yard. Kids these days, they thought they were the center of the universe, Tommy huffed. Another day, another time, he would have taught the boy a lesson right then and there.

Tommy whistled as he walked. It was a good day, but then, at his age, any day that he woke up was a good day.

Chapter Five

How to ride a horse: Step One – Mount the horse.
Step Two – Stay mounted!

"Maggie hasn't come down yet," Sam asked, washing his hands at the kitchen sink before he sat down to supper.

"Not yet," Emma replied, depositing a plate of fish and chips in front of Sam's place at the head of the table.

"Yeah, fish sticks," Jenny cried out as she slipped into her seat beside Mary.

"I love them too," Mary grinned, stealing one of Jenny's fish sticks and biting into it.

"Hey," Jenny laughed, stealing a fish stick from Mary's plate in retaliation.

"I'm starved," BJ added, taking a seat beside his grandfather after returning from cleaning up in the downstairs bathroom.

"Cole says he's looking forward to Sunday dinner, Emma," Zoe said, squirting a mound of ketchup on the plate beside her French fries.

"That boy can sure pack it away," Sylvie chuckled. "You better go slaughter one of those steers of yours before the weekend, Sam."

"Might have to," Sam chortled.

"Wait a minute, when did you see Cole and what were you doing with my boyfriend," Emma joked, pointing a fork menacingly at Zoe.

"Now you're in trouble," Sylvie whispered to the red faced woman sitting beside her.

"Oh, I ran into him this morning," Zoe blurted out, trying unsuccessfully to sound innocent.

"And where was that," Emma pressed her.

"Alongside the interstate on the way to see Tommy," Zoe shrugged, picking up a French fry and studiously studying it.

"It ain't gonna change shape until you bite into it," Sylvie elbowed her friend.

Zoe glared at Sylvie and bit the top off the potato wedge.

Sam put down his fork and raised an eyebrow.

Zoe and Sylvie both shrugged, raising their eyebrows back at him, daring him to question Zoe further.

Maggie clumped down the stairs and swished into the kitchen in a flowery sarong. Her hair was tied on top of her head with two Japanese chop sticks. Maggie's face was flushed as if she had just stepped out of the bath.

Sylvie suspected she had, needing to sober up before descending the stairs. She had to admit, she was worried for Maggie. Her friend had been drinking a lot lately and it needed to stop. Even before their words this afternoon,

Maggie had taken to drinking the hard stuff in the afternoon instead of her usual glass of wine or two at dinner or before bed.

"Saved by the belle," Zoe quipped, enjoying the pun.

"Maggie," Sam grunted, nodding towards the irritating woman.

"Sam," she replied, slipping into the empty seat on the far side of Zoe.

"I'll get your dinner," Emma said, glowering at her father-in-law. "I put it in the oven to keep warm in case you weren't up to eating until later."

"Thank you," Maggie replied regally as Emma placed a plate full of fish sticks and French fries on the table in front of her. "What kind of fish is this?"

"White fish," Sylvie countered, leaning forward for a better view of the illustrious Maggie Carroll.

"Lovely," Maggie said, tipping her head ever so slightly towards Sylvie.

Sylvie grinned crookedly, knowing how much her girlfriend hated boxed frozen fish sticks. She waited for the rebuff to spring from Maggie's lips, but it never came. Score one for Mags, Sylvie thought, impressed.

"It's Atlantic Cod," Emma added, retaking her seat at the dinner table.

"It's scrumpty-delicious," Jenny piped in.

"And best eaten with a squeeze of lemon," Mary purred.

"And a dollop of homemade tartar sauce," Emma grinned.

"Amen," Sam finished.

The group at the table turned in mid-supper and stared.

"What? You think I can't play that game," Sam quipped.

Everyone around the table laughed.

"So, Zoe, how did you run into Cole," Emma continued. "You never said."

Zoe blushed. Maggie glanced sideways at her rival, and remained mute.

"She got a ticket," Sylvie said, slapping her knee, as the image of Zoe in her little black beamer being pulled over by the sheriff sprang into her mind.

"You ladies got to learn that life in the fast lane has consequences," Sam mumbled.

Sylvie slapped Sam playfully on the shoulder.

Sam harrumphed and remained as silent as Maggie.

Emma, Sylvie and Mary exchanged a knowing look while BJ, Zoe and Maggie tucked into their dinner.

Jenny was Jenny and animatedly regaled them with the teacher's stories about donkey racing and Jenny's plans to enter the donkey race with Mike.

Eventually Jenny ran out of steam and Emma cleared the plates from the table.

"I'm guessing you're looking for sponsors," Sylvie commented dryly.

"Yes, please," Jenny beamed, "as soon as I get my sign up sheet. You can sponsor me by the mile or as a lump sum. Oh, by the way, Mom, it costs ten dollars for me to enter the race, is that okay?"

"Of course it is, baby," Emma agreed, placing six coffee cups and a full coffee urn on the table. "It's Mike that I'm worried about."

"Mike and me have four weeks to train," Jenny chattered on. "We can do it and they got vet checks every mile so if he can't finish the five miles, I'm okay with that."

"That's very wise of you," Mary agreed.

"You want to run with me, Mary? I bet we can find you a donkey at the rescue?"

"I think I'd rather cheer you on from the sidelines," the retired barrel racer replied.

Sam guffawed.

Sylvie smacked him again.

"You keep hitting me, I'm gonna have to teach you a lesson," Sam grumbled.

"That's the idea," Sylvie teased, a glint in her eye.

Sam shook his head in exasperation as he poured himself and Sylvie a cup of coffee.

"We'll all be there to cheer you on, Jenny" Mary smiled.

"On the subject of asses, I've been told that I have been a bit of one," Maggie declared, silencing everyone.

When nobody argued, she continued, "Apparently, I owe you an apology, Sam, and you as well, Emma. I promise I won't do it again."

"That's good of you, Maggie," Emma nodded. "Isn't it Sam?"

Everyone at the table, except for Jenny, turned to look at contemplative man. Jenny munched away at a fish stick like she was a beaver sawing a log.

"Fair enough," he replied after a moment.

"I don't think you're an ass, Miss Carroll," Jenny quipped, licking her fingers. "Your stallion is though."

Maggie's mouth dropped open. The rest of the ladies covered their mouths to keep from laughing aloud.

"Jenny Montana, you go wash your mouth out with soap," Emma half-scolded her daughter, her own eyes watering as she suppressed a laugh.

"But I haven't had my pie yet," the little girl whined.

Emma plucked Jenny up by the ear and escorted her out of the kitchen.

"She's right," Sylvie laughed, checking to make sure Jenny was out of ear shot.

"Yes, I know, Storm is an ass," Maggie agreed.

"Stubborn as one," Mary agreed.

"He would look good with pink ribbons in his hair though, don't you think," Zoe added, reminding the ladies of Jenny's dress up days with Mike. The aged donkey would flatten his one and only ear back in disdain when Jenny approached with the intent to decorate. It always involved pink… lots of pink.

BJ's face turned as crimson as the cherries in the cherry pie that sat on the table beside a lemon meringue pie.

"On that note, I'm going to cut me a piece of that lemon pie," Sam said, reaching across the table to pull one of the pies towards him.

"Not on your life," Sylvie cried, also reaching for the pie.

The pie skittered sideways, almost falling to the floor, but Sam caught it at the last minute, the fresh meringue splattering him in the eye.

"Ooops," Sylvie grinned.

Sam scooped the meringue off his face with one finger, picked up his fork, dipped it into the pie and flung a forkful of meringue at Sylvie.

There was a gasp of surprise from all around the table.

Mary picked up a teaspoon and eyed BJ.

"Oh, no you don't," BJ roared, snatching another teaspoon off the table. He dipped the spoon into the lemon meringue pie and faced Mary like Doc Holiday facing the Clanton brothers at the OK Corral.

Zoe and Maggie grinned evilly and picked up their own teaspoons.

Mary let the pie fly. It glanced off BJ's chin. BJ launched his own catapult. The white meringue hit Mary in the forehead, catching in her bangs and dangling down her face like a Christmas ornament.

Pandemonium erupted!

"What in the devil is going on here," Emma hollered, walking back into the kitchen with a baleful child at her side.

Sam, BJ, and the ladies looked up through meringue spattered hair and faces. The pie that Emma had slaved over that morning was bare topped, the lemon gelatine wobbling atop the pastry, the meringue everywhere but where it was supposed to be.

"Nothing," Sam grinned.

"Don't even think about it," Emma warned him.

Sam dipped his spoon into the lemon gelatine and flung it at his daughter-in-law. It splattered across her nose and right cheek.

"You are so going to regret that, Sam Montana," Emma growled, wiping the lemon from her face. She walked purposefully over to the table and picked up the trashed pie.

"Oh, oh," BJ snorted, scrambling out of the way.

"What'd I miss," Jenny sniffled.

"The grand finale," Emma purred, slamming the pie into Sam's face.

***

The women laughed and joked as they helped Emma clean up the kitchen while Sam and BJ went out to tend to the horses.

Sylvie and Emma smiled at each other as Zoe and Maggie took bets as to which of their stallions would take a chunk out of the boys' shirts once they got a sniff of the sugar in the meringue that coated their hair and clothes.

The pie fight had done wonders to ease the tension in the household.

Sylvie nudged Emma.

Emma nudged Sylvie back.

Sylvie picked up a pie plate. There was still a smidgeon of pie left in it.

"Doooonnnn't," Emma warned the older woman.

Sylvie grinned, a wicked gleam in her eyes, her mouth curving into a joker's grin.

Chapter Six

Horse… If God made anything more beautiful he kept it for himself!

The snow on the mountain tops sparkled in the distance, the slopes alive with colourful wild flowers as spring caused the long sloping pastures below them to green up. The Montana's cattle grazed close to the fenced lane leading up to the ranch. The creek that ran through the middle of the ranch was more a rushing river than the gentle flowing stream that it was the rest of the year.

Sam stood at the gate of the first newly fenced grass paddock, the sun shining down on his sweat stained Stetson, his hazel eyes fixed upon Zoe as she led the pregnant Andalusian filly to her new turn-out. The filly's coat glistened, the grey dapples fading as her coat turned white, her belly widening as the mare's pregnancy progressed. The filly had been accidentally bred last summer when Maggie's flashy sorrel stallion escaped during a cougar attack. Extravaganza, like her owner, was a stunning sight to behold.

Right behind the trim figure of Zoe in her custom made breaches and riding jacket, strolled his grandson in his worn boots and blue jeans leading Zoe's prancing white Andalusian stallion, Zippo. BJ had been riding the aged stallion under Zoe's tutelage for nine months. The teen and the stallion had formed a real bond so much so that BJ didn't need to use a stallion chain with the stud anymore. The horse was attuned to BJ's every move.

The ranch horses in the pasture with the cattle whinnied at the approach of the stallion. Sam's reining horse, Checkers, a red and white paint, squealed, as did Penny, Emma's bay Quarter horse, and Jenny's little Appaloosa pony, Rosie, as the stallion drew nearer. Sam wasn't surprised. Zippo was a fine specimen.

The stallion proudly arched his neck and shook his elegant long white mane. It was as pretty a sight as Niagara Falls. The Andalusian snorted, his brown eyes taking in the mares interest. Sam didn't think it was possible, but the stud puffed up even more.

"The mares are going to be carrying on for awhile," Sam grinned as he opened the gate for Zoe and the filly.

"And so they should," Zoe purred. "You're never too old for love, Sam."

"Yes, ma'am," Sam nodded.

"I don't want Extravaganza to get too worked up though," Zoe added, worry creasing her brow.

"Don't worry, BJ and me will be staying out here until they all settle down," Sam consoled her. "We won't let anything happen to that filly and her baby."

"I'll hold you to that, young man," Zoe smirked.

"Young man, is it?" Sam chortled. The age difference between him and Zoe was only a few months. "Keep that halter on her and hold her by the gate until everyone is out."

Zoe nodded as Sam closed and locked the gate behind her.

BJ walked past him, his blue eyes alight with happiness as the stallion dipped his head toward the boy's shoulder and snuffled his hair gently.

"I'd sure love to breed this big guy to Checkers or Bonny," BJ whispered in passing.

"Like I said, I'll think about it," Sam answered, motioning BJ forward.

Sam waved to Mary and his granddaughter waiting patiently in the outside paddock behind the barn. Jenny pushed open the gate and tugged Mike through it. Mary followed after Jenny with her paint stallion, Patch, a handsome sixteen hand twenty-five year-old bay overo paint with blue eyes. The donkey sensed the energy in the air and walked forward quickly when it realized they were heading in the opposite direction of the barn and the house.

The two geldings, Bucky, BJ's buckskin cutting horse, and Sam's retired reining horse, Boomer, trotted to the fence, their eyes wide at the parade of stallions as Sylvie left the barn, her gigantic Hanoverian stallion, Midnight Special, aka Buddy, walked quietly beside her. The slightly hammer headed bay stallion towered over its slim owner. The stallion was so gentle and even tempered that Sam wondered why people weren't lining up to breed their mares to him, despite the stud's retirement from the world of hunters.

The last stallion to leave the barn was Desert Storm, the elegant sorrel Trakehner with a snippet of white on its forehead and four white socks. Sam quietly wondered if Maggie's nasty temperament had rubbed off on the stud. Both of them were stubborn and hot tempered; although, she had been trying to be nicer the past few days.

Storm was the only horse with a stallion chain wrapped firmly around its nose. Maggie also carried a long handled dressage whip in one hand.

Sam had to admit, Maggie handled the stallion expertly. Until the ladies arrived at the ranch with the stallions, Sam believed women shouldn't handle studs, but each and every one of these women had proven him wrong.

A green GMC truck pulled into the yard as Sylvie flicked the end of the lead rope at Sam's bottom as she sashayed by him.

"Who's that," she asked, skipping out of the way before Sam could swat her bottom in return.

"Ranger Dee," BJ replied leaning over Zippo's gate, his face breaking into a school boy grin.

"I hope there isn't another rogue cougar running around," Mary fretted, slowing her pace.

Buddy's stride was so long that he quickly overtook Jenny and Mary.

"Don't worry, Patch and the Bulldozers will protect you," Jenny quipped.

The mares next door continued to squeal and squirt as the four-legged parade of testosterone walked by, necks arched, nostrils flared as the studs scented the girls.

The two Saint Bernards ran out to greet the ranger as the pretty brunette stepped out of the truck. She hunkered down and gave each dog a kiss, a pat, and a treat, in that order.

"Well, she ain't in her ranger uniform so it ain't an official visit," Sam drawled.

Emma raced out of the house, across the yard, and embraced Dee in a bear hug. The two women laughed, broke apart, and then started walking towards Sam and the others.

"Okay, move along everyone," Sam waved.

As soon as Mike spied the open gate to his new pen and the luscious grass inside, he charged forward, yanking Jenny off her feet.

"Mike, you're naughty," Jenny scolded the donkey, a look of betrayal on her face.

Mary stopped to help Jenny to her feet. Jenny threw her arms around the old woman's waist and hugged her, tears flowing.

"Chin up," the agreeable woman said. "Mike didn't mean to ditch you, he was just excited."

"Are you sure," Jenny whined, breaking away from the woman she called her cowgirl grandma.

"I'm sure," Mary assured the child.

The ranch geldings snorted and jogged back and forth along the fence line as the mares continued to work themselves into a lathered tizzy.

51

Sam groaned. He expected all three mares would be in heat by day's end. No matter their age, race, creed or kind, women fell hard for a good looking male.

"Look out," Dee hollered as Maggie's stallion predictably exploded as it approached the paddock where BJ stood leaning against the gate, the Andalusian stallion at his side suddenly deciding to challenge the other stud's approach by pawing the earth.

Storm reared and lashed out with his front hooves, dragging Maggie forward and into the air, the stud chain snapping taut.

"Move Zippo back," Sam yelled at BJ as he raced to Maggie's aid.

Ahead of him, Mary slammed Patch and Mike's gate shut with an audible thud. Sylvie followed suit in Buddy's paddock.

"Back," BJ ordered the Andalusian stallion, placing a hand on the stud's chest and pushing him backwards with one hand while tightening his hold on the halter with the other. Zippo pinned his ears and snapped his teeth at the chestnut stallion, but responded to BJ's aids.

"Oh, Zippo, you should be used to that fool hothead by now," Zoe chortled, rolling her eyes at Maggie's charging stallion while her filly squealed nervously and sidestepped away from her. Zoe shook out the lead line and pointed at the mare, using a natural horsemanship technique to drive the horse's body backwards and away from the distractions. The filly tried to ignore her, but Zoe increased the force of her movements until she had the filly's complete attention and the horse responded.

"I've got this," Maggie growled at Sam, tugging wickedly on the chain around her stallion's nose to bring him back down to earth while tapping the dressage whip against his shoulder to move him away from the gate. She instantly released the pressure when he stepped sideways and brought his head down.

"Maggie," Sam muttered, skidding to a stop in front of her.

"Like I said, 'I've got this'," the raven haired woman snapped.

Maggie tapped the dressage whip on the ground three times. The sorrel stallion snorted, tried to rear again, but she gave him one sharp tug on the chain and scooted him forward. He danced briefly on the spot and then settled into an elevated walk beside his confident owner.

"Well, I guess she told him," Dee chuckled as she approached Sam and BJ.

"Glad I don't have to handle that nitwit," Emma agreed.

"Wait, until we release them all," BJ laughed. "That should be fun."

"Define fun, grandson," Sam grimaced as he strode quickly after Maggie.

"You come to see the action," Mary yelled, waving at Dee.

"That and to see if BJ wants to help me lay out the Donkey Race Course," Dee waved back.

"Really," BJ squirmed, causing Zippo to raise his head and scream out his presence.

"Yep, I got a lot of flagging to do," Dee nodded.

"I told Dee you would be more than happy to volunteer," Emma added, leaning over the fence to pat Zippo.

"I'm in," the boy agreed.

"Okay, everyone, we're gonna let Storm loose first and then Patch and Mike, then Buddy, and Zippo. Zoe, you hold on to Extravaganza until the boys settle down a bit." Sam yelled from the far paddock.

"No problem, Sam," Zoe called back.

Sam went into the paddock with Maggie. If the stud freaked out and turned to lash out prior to being set free, he wanted to deal with it. He wasn't going to take 'no' for an answer.

"I'll take it from here, Maggie," he said, taking the lead rope from her hands.

"I am quite capable of releasing my own horse," she seethed.

"Yep, but my ranch, my responsibility," Sam replied simply.

Maggie stomped away. She stopped by the gate and waited.

"Out," he reiterated.

"Fine," she spat, leaving the paddock.

So much for her change of heart, Sam grinned.

"Easy big guy," Sam said, rubbing a hand down the stud's sweaty neck. "I know, you're as high strung as your momma, but you don't have to be. Ya hear me?"

The stallion licked his lips and lowered his head to Sam. Sam tugged the stud's head towards him and slowly slipped off the halter, keeping the lead line around his neck so the stud wouldn't whirl around and kick out. A cowboy buddy of his had been killed that way after a hind hoof had connected with his head. The sorrel stood quietly for a moment, lowered his head and nibbled on the grass.

Sam let out his breath, slipped the rope from around Storm's neck and backed away, keeping a cautious eye on the stallion.

"Well that went better than expected," he sighed, exiting the paddock.

"Of course it did," Maggie remarked. She was about to say something snide, but then thought better of it.

At least she was trying, Sam mused...for the moment, at any rate.

Sam waved to Sylvie to let Buddy go. Sylvie slipped off the big bay's halter and he wandered a few feet, laid down in the grass and started to roll.

Mary helped Jenny with Mike's halter, the donkey deciding that the grass was greener anywhere but where the little girl was standing, and then let her paint horse loose.

"So far, it's been pretty quiet," Emma said to Sam as he walked with Maggie back along the fence line. "That's impressive. I thought there would be more aerial leaps."

"I expect it's the calm before the storm," Sam quipped.

"And don't forget the girls," Dee chuckled.

"They're in love," Sylvie laughed.

"Okay, BJ," Sam waved to his grandson.

BJ unfastened the latch on the halter and let go of the white stallion. Zippo trotted away and lay down in the grass to roll too.

"This is seriously uneventful," Zoe whined. "I'm just going to let Extravaganza go."

"Maybe you should wait a few minutes and walk her around," Sam urged Zoe.

As soon as he said it, the donkey named Mike trotted over to the fence and tried to sniff his uppity new neighbour. He then let out a great loud bray in greeting.

Storm leapt straight into the air like a Halloween cat and bolted across the pasture, bucking like a young colt as his hooves dug into the soft ground.

The paint lifted his head, whinnied and then barrelled down the fence line at a break neck speed. At the last minute, the stallion put on the brakes, tucking in his butt in an award winning slide, and then reversed direction, running back to the gate at break neck speed.

The red stallion followed suit, except for the slide. Instead, he tucked his head deep into his chest and galloped a figure eight, returning to where he started.

Buddy and Zippo joined in, galloping up and down their fence lines, tails in the air, hooves above the ground, their elevated movements a joy to behold.

The two Saint Bernards bolted past the group of awestruck people standing in the grass alleyway between the ranch horses and the new pens, barking furiously. It was all in a day's fun after all.

"Eeeekkkk," Zoe yelled as the pregnant filly let out a buck and jogged after the boys, tail in the air, mane flying, pirouetting in mid stride.

The ranch horses raced off, startling the cattle into a stampede.

"Good grief," Sam grumbled, tipping his cowboy hat back on his head as the ground shook beneath his feet.

"Someone was saying they wanted to see some action," Sylvie laughed.

Dee pulled her cell phone out of her pocket and started snapping pictures.

"Patch has still got it," Mary cooed slipping her arm under Jenny's.

"Look at Mike, he's running," Jenny hollered gleefully. "We're going to win that donkey race."

"I bet you will," Sylvie high-fived the little girl. "Look at that ole donkey go!"

"My filly," Zoe moaned.

"She'll be fine," Dee consoled the distraught woman. "Look, she's already settling down."

"You'd settle down too if you were carrying that load around," Emma grinned. "I feel her pain."

Extravaganza stopped and snorted in excitement, her eyes bright. The filly shook her head, her glossy silver mane rippling.

"Gosh, she's beautiful," Jenny gushed.

"She is that," Zoe agreed, relaxing as the filly's front legs crumpled beneath her and the horse started to roll.

"I'm going to have an awful lot of grooming to do tonight," BJ moaned as the grass stains on the white horses' rumps and shoulders got bigger and bigger the more they rolled.

"Yeah, but that's after you help me out," Dee elbowed the teen.

BJ blushed.

Sam thought his grandson was going to faint. He'd had a crush on Dee for as long as Sam could remember.

***

Dee swung off the highway and onto the dirt side road that wound its way up to the rocky mesa studded with scrub pine and dirty mounds of snow on the lower reaches of the mountain range that bordered the long narrow valley that encapsulated the Diamond Bar, Montana family spread, and numerous other ranches in the area. The road was a busy thorough fare in the spring and summer for mountain bikers, hikers, and horseback riders alike. In the fall, hunters used it to ATV into the high country.

The GMC truck splashed through the deep puddles the winter run-off had caused, some of them large enough to rip out a muffler.

"What a great place to run the race," BJ said, one hand on top of the cab to protect himself as the truck bounced through a particularly large pothole.

"I think so too," Dee agreed. "We are a mile in now. I thought I'd ask Terry at the town hall if he could run the grader over the beat up sections of the road before the race starts."

"There's lots of parking along the highway as well," BJ grinned.

"And lots of places to set up water stations and checkpoints," Dee nodded, her eyes on the road.

"You figure the old mine is about half way?" BJ queried his eyes on the mountain pass ahead of them.

58

"Yep. The race committee decided to do ten miles this year instead of twenty-five. If it's a success, they'll go bigger next year."

BJ and Dee rode in silence for awhile, Dee focused on driving, having had to slip the truck into four-by-four as the road got muddier. Ahead of them, rain clouds hung low in the mountains, threatening to put an end to the lovely spring day.

The truck's transmission ground loudly as Dee shifted gears. It startled a couple of white tailed deer. They scampered up the rocky slope as Dee slowed to watch them, a smile sweeping across her face. The deer weren't fat, but they weren't overly skinny either, their coats splotchy as their winter coats moulted away.

"I think you better get your transmission serviced before the race," BJ stammered.

"This old gal's been doing that for years," Dee laughed lightly.

The truck rounded a bend.

Several tattered buildings were nestled against the lower slope of the mountain. They fought to remain standing against the onslaught of Father Time. There was the remnants of an old stable, the black smith forge visible through the broken wooden slats of weathered boards, a two storey hotel with gaping holes in the front porch, an old saloon whose doors were missing and front windows broken, plus a surveyor's office with a collapsed roof.

"There's a big old corral behind the stable that won't take much fixing up. We can use it for the vet check station and trailers turn around for runners that only do the first leg of the race," Dee pointed, pulling the truck up in front of the saloon.

"So this is five miles," BJ asked.

"It is. This will be the end of the kids section of the race," Dee answered. "We'll place some barricades up in front of the buildings to keep folks out. I was concerned about stopping here at first, but it's quite the back drop for a donkey race, don't you think?"

"Yeah, this place is cool," BJ agreed. "Did it ever have a name?"

"I'm sure it did, but like so many of these places, its name has been lost to time. We rangers call it 'Lost Dreams'. There are all sorts of men buried in the cemetery on the hill who'd probably agree."

"It must have been a crazy place in its heyday," BJ whistled.

"The mine is another two miles up the wagon trail. I rode to it last week. The trail is wide open so we'll do the whole loop and you can tell me what you think. There's a ranger station over to the north, but that is at the foot of the back country and I didn't want folks to have to back track over the same trail."

"At least, we don't have to tag much," BJ grinned. "All the locals know this place."

"Yeah, it's the forest road on the way down from the mine that will need the most flagging," Dee agreed. "We still have to remember there will be out-of-towners coming that may never have been here before."

"I didn't think about that. Is Gus going to help?" BJ asked quietly.

"Gus is away catching bad guys," the ranger grinned. "If he can, he said that he'd help out on race day."

"Oh," BJ mumbled, his face betraying his emotions.

Gus Rodriquez was Dee's boyfriend. He was a hot ATF agent and one of BJ's father's best friends. BJ's father had been killed overseas while on his first tour of duty. Gus had lost touch with the family until he suddenly showed up at the ranch, spearheading the search for Tommy Cortez last summer.

A smattering of rain hit the windshield.

"Time to pitter-patter," Dee joked, throwing the truck into gear.

A loud 'thunk' issued from the GMC's gear box as Dee flipped the four by four into low gear before starting the climb up the narrow wagon trail to the mine. The rain that had been threatening to fall began in earnest. The truck's tracks were quickly washed away.

Chapter Seven

Who needs men when you have a horse?..oh..wait..someone's gotta do the paying!

Tommy was sipping on a coffee in the mess hall when a bandy legged balding inmate with a red nose, grey eyes, and devil-may-care strut sat down on the bench across from him. He had seen the guy around, but couldn't remember his name.

"I just wanted to stop and congratulate you," the grey haired man grinned. "It ain't often we get a wedding around here. Seriously, when I heard about it, my spirits soared. I was in a pretty dark place. You know what I mean?"

Tommy remained silent.

Undaunted, the man continued, his blue eyes dazzlingly bright.

"I hear your gal's quite the looker and has horses," he babbled. "I used to have horses. Thoroughbreds. The sport of kings. There ain't nothing like standing beside your colt in the winner's circle."

Still, Tommy didn't respond, hoping the guy would get the drift. The guy should know better. He was about Tommy's age and had the jaundiced look of a lifer. Still, Tommy supposed he could afford to be civil.

A couple of Tommy's men stood up, their faces and bodies taut, ready for a fight.

Tommy raised a hand.

The men sat back down.

"That's what put me in here," the old man continued, oblivious to the danger he was in. "When ya ain't supposed to win, ya don't."

"How much time ya done?" Tommy asked.

"I got three weeks left," the orange clad inmate grinned, ducking the actual question. "Don't know what I'm gonna do. The wife and the lawyer cleaned me out. I got a brother out there I haven't talked to in fifty years. I'm hoping he can help me out."

One of the guards walked over and leaned over to whisper in Tommy's ear, "You got a visitor."

Tommy nodded and stood up.

"Anyways, congratulations," the dandy stuttered, offering Tommy his hand.

Tommy stood up, turning his back on the unwanted interloper. The guy seemed harmless enough. Word was out. There had been a lot of back slapping in the past few days. The guards had let the cat out of the bag.

The former crime lord stalked across the dining hall, the worst of the worst nodding to him as he passed them by.

Tommy walked beside the guard. He glanced back. The strange old lifer was watching him, a calculated look on his face: it made the hair rise on the back of Tommy' neck. He would have to ask around about him.

A handsome black haired young man with olive skin and deep set brown eyes waited at a table inside the communal visiting area. Tommy was rarely allowed in here given the nature of his crimes. The thirty year-old man wore a crisp white t-shirt and black jeans tucked over an expensive pair of black leather boots.

"JJ," Tommy grinned, sitting down at the table.

"Pops, you look good," Tommy's son grinned back.

Two more guards came in and stood discreetly off to one side, hands resting on their hips.

"You look good too," Tommy nodded approval. "When are you going to settle down and give me some more grandchildren?"

"Unlike you, I haven't met the right woman yet," JJ smiled. "Apparently, I'm not the stud my father is."

The guards behind them smothered a laugh.

JJ scowled.

"Don't mind them, they're just jealous," Tommy chuckled. "So, did you get it?"

"I did," JJ replied, tugging a blue velvet ring case from his pocket. He popped the lid and handed the case to his father. It contained a round two carat brilliant cut diamond ring. "I could have gone bigger, but you said the lady had small hands."

Tommy broke into a wide grin.

"This is perfect," the craggy faced old man sniffed, holding the diamond up to the light. It glittered like frost under a full moon.

The guards leaned forward for a better look.

"Now that's a rock," the older guard whistled.

"We're in the wrong business," the younger guard muttered.

"You know we might have to confiscate that," the guard that brought Tommy in stammered.

"No, you don't. I bought it myself," JJ spat, glaring at the guard. "It's my wedding gift to my father and his fiancée."

"Yeah? And where'd you get that kind of money," the guard continued, casting a worried look back and forth between Tommy, JJ, and the other guards.

"Hey, I'm a mechanic," JJ said, flashing a beatific smile at the guards. "It's a license to make money."

The guards roared with laughter.

"I did good?" JJ asked, turning back to his father.

"You did good, son," Tommy whispered, wiping his eyes. "Zoe's going to love it."

Tommy reached over the table and hugged his son.

"Tommy," the largest of the guards said, stepping forward.

"I know, I know," Tommy replied, leaning back.

"I booked into a hotel for a few days," JJ said, taking back the ring case.

"Bueno, I'll call Zoe and ask her to come tomorrow afternoon," Tommy sighed happily. "The warden okayed the extra visit. Can you come back then?"

"Of course, I can," JJ beamed. "Anything for you, papa."

***

Benny drove his rusted white Bronco over the rutted road, the monotonous drone of the windshield wipers reverberating through the cab. The Bronco bumped along, the suspension groaning. Percy held onto the handle above the passenger side door, his seat belt cutting into his abdomen.

The rain fell in sheets. A river of muddy water ran down the center of the gravel road. The top of the mountain before them was shrouded in heavy black clouds.

Percy bit his lip. He wondered how he'd let Benny talk him into this. Why did he have to always go along with him? It had always been like that. Ever since they were kids, Percy had allowed Benny to make all the important decisions for him. Both their fathers were doing time, just in different penitentiaries.

Percy looked through the grime and rain streaked window as they pulled up to the once thriving mining town. It was hard to imagine the thousands of gold miners who had come and gone through this little town, living in tents, wallowing in the mud, getting drunk in the saloon. If the men were lucky, they'd take their gold and leave quickly. If not, they got rolled and robbed, or worse, were murdered and buried in the sad cemetery on the hill.

Percy had a bad feeling about all of this.

Benny pulled up in front of the two story hotel.

"What are we doing here," Percy asked.

"This is it," Benny grinned, turning off the engine. "I've been looking around for a week. This is the best place."

"Here?" Percy's voice warbled as he stared out the window at the rickety buildings.

"Yeah, come on," Benny urged his friend. "You aren't scared of a little rain, are you?"

Percy closed his eyes momentarily.

It wasn't too late. He could back out now, couldn't he?

Benny slugged him in the arm and then pushed open the Bronco's door.

Percy sighed and followed suit.

"This way," Benny yelled over the sound of the drumming rain.

Percy flipped his collar up as the rain pelted him in the face. He chased after Benny, racing around the back of the ratty hotel.

A rusted metal "Danger - Do Not Enter" sign was posted on the back door of the former hotel. It was peppered with bullet holes. There were no windows, just a solid wall of weathered boards, silvered with age. Benny ripped the sign off its pegs and shouldered open the flimsy wooden door. He walked over the threshold and disappeared into the blackness within.

Percy coughed on the dust as he entered the abandoned hotel. He heard a skittering in the darkness. Rats! Percy hated rats.

"Benny, where the heck, are you," he called after his partner.

"In here," Benny replied.

Percy pulled out his apartment keys and flicked on the small penlight that dangled from the key chain. He instantly wished he hadn't. Huge wolf spiders hung from spider webs along the ceiling and the doorway. Husks of dead flies and other bugs bounced in the webs from the draft coming from the open doorway behind him. Mouse and rat droppings littered the floor.

Floor boards creaked menacingly beneath his sneakers. A broken leg was the last thing he needed.

"Frigging radical, partner," Benny said, emerging through the doorway.

No, it wasn't frigging radical, Percy grimaced.

"This way," Benny motioned him onwards. Benny's brown eyes looked like cat's eyes in the penlight's thin beam and the spiked blond streaks in his hair made him look like something out of a bad horror movie.

Percy didn't like this, not one little bit. Still, he followed along like an obedient puppy. Percy hated himself for doing it.

The two young men slumped into the kitchen. There was a grease covered woodstove with a broken pipe leading outside, a counter with a hole in it that looked like it might fit a tin wash tub, a walk in pantry lined with rickety shelves, and a window cut into one wall which led into a rectangular shaped dining room. There were only two windows, one in the kitchen and one in the side dining room wall, both covered in cracked yellowed oil skin. The windows in the front of the building were mostly boarded up but you could still see some daylight beyond them and the front of the Bronco's grill. Several broken tables and chairs were strewn about.

"We can hide the broads in here," Benny boomed. "You'll have to stay with them. We'll pick up a couple of camp lanterns and sleeping bags. We can tie them to the stove. There's no way they can break free of that. It must weigh two hundred pounds."

Percy's eyes widened with fear.

Stay here?

In the mountains?

With the rats and two old ladies?

Was Benny nuts?

"Yeah, okay," Percy squeaked in response.

"Righteous! It's all coming together, bro," Benny said, a spark of madness in his eyes.

Percy didn't think it was 'all coming together' at all. In fact, he felt like he was going to be sick.

"Exactly where are you gonna be," he casually asked his friend.

"Me? Where do you think? Someone's gotta deal with collecting the money. You gonna do it? I don't think so," Benny hissed. "We're gonna be rich, bro."

"Yeah, rich," Percy winced as the wind hit the building with increasing force, shaking it to its very foundation.

Chapter Eight

Life is like a wild horse. You ride it or it rides you.

Zoe floated into kitchen as if she walked on air, a dazzlingly bright smile on her face, accompanied by a fellow who looked like he had just stepped out of one of those fashion magazines that Maggie subscribed to. It was impossible to miss the gigantic rock on Zoe's finger.

What on earth?

Emma turned from carving the baked ham on the counter and laughed with childish glee. She stopped in mid-swipe and raced over to Zoe, wiping her hands on her apron as she did so. Emma immediately lifted Zoe's hand and examined the ring, cooing like a baby.

"Sir," the young man said politely, offering Sam is hand.

"And you are," Sam asked, shaking the man's outstretched hand.

At least the swarthy brigand in designer jeans, shirt and boots, was polite.

"Miss Zoe," Jenny yelled, racing across the kitchen to see the ring her mother was going gaga over. "Are you getting married?"

"Hells-bells," Sam muttered, levelling a 'did you know about this?' look at Emma. Emma shook her head in the negative.

"I hope it's to this handsome young man," Mary kidded, getting up from the table.

"No, ma'am, although I'd be honoured," JJ Cortez bowed, lifting Mary's hand for a kiss.

"Ooooh, I like you," Mary giggled.

"Tommy asked me to marry him and I said 'yes'," Zoe purred. "Oh, my, where are my manners. This is JJ, Tommy's son."

"Ladies," he bowed elegantly, his dark brown eyes taking in Sam's lovely daughter-in-law. "I am sorry that we arrived at dinner. I didn't mean to intrude."

"Oh, you aren't intruding at all," Emma blushed, her eyes finally leaving the ring and settling on the pirate king.

Sam wasn't a happy man. He'd seen this young man's type before. The fact that he bared a considerable resemblance to Gus Rodriquez who Emma had a crush on for awhile last year didn't go unnoticed.

"Have you eaten," Emma stammered. "We have lots."

"Oh, do stay for dinner, JJ," Zoe beseeched him.

"I'd love to if I'm not putting you out."

"You can take my seat," Jenny offered. "I'll grab a fold up chair from the back and sit between Mom and Mary."

Jenny rushed to the living room without checking with Sam or Emma that it was okay. Sam wasn't as amused as everyone else.

BJ came down the stairs, fresh out of the shower, Maggie coming down after him.

"What's all the commotion," Maggie grumbled, her hair swept up in a luxurious wave atop her head. She wore a knee length red silk kimono tied over black slacks. She stopped short when she caught sight of Zoe holding up her hand, the giant diamond on Zoe's ring finger impossible to miss. Her composure crumbled, but then she lifted her chin and smirked.

"You didn't actually say 'yes'," Maggie muttered through clenched teeth.

"I did," Zoe replied, lifting her own chin in the air.

Good grief, Sam glowered, here comes the fireworks.

It took a moment for Maggie to re-group, but she surprised Sam when she walked stiff backed to her seat at the table and sat down, folding her hands demurely in her lap.

BJ looked completely befuddled as he took his seat beside Sam while Jenny dragged a chair into the kitchen. Mary helped Jenny find another place setting and they both settled down.

"You must be Maggie Carroll," JJ remarked, striding over to Maggie. He picked up her hand and kissed it gently.

Sam and Sylvie both snorted in amusement.

Maggie blushed as JJ held out the last empty chair for Zoe. Zoe slipped into it, a sly grin on her face, as she flashed the diamond in Maggie's face.

"Sit," Sam commanded the engaging young man.

"Thank you, sir," JJ replied politely, taking a seat. "It isn't often that I get to eat a homemade family dinner. My brother, sister and I live quite a ways apart so we only see each other on holidays."

"And weddings," Zoe quipped.

"Yes, and special occasions," JJ agreed.

"And what do you do for a living," Mary asked as Emma placed a plate of sliced ham on the table, Emma's eyes fixed on the handsome son of a notorious gangster.

Sam almost growled, but Sylvie kicked him lightly under the table. Their eyes met. Sylvie reminded him of Annie Potts, Sheldon's feisty grandmother on Young Sheldon.

"JJ's a mechanic," Zoe chirped. "He has his own garage and everything."

"You a good one?" Sam queried, raising an eyebrow.

"The best," JJ smiled.

"Oooh, do you fix tractors," Emma marvelled. "Our big one is acting up, isn't it, Sam?"

"Nothing BJ and I can't handle," Sam shrugged, helping himself to a heaping spoonful of scalloped potatoes.

BJ shot him a questioning look.

"Don't forget your peas, boy," Sam said to his grandson.

BJ was smart enough to read between the lines.

Sam glanced around the table at all the blushing women. They reminded him of the mares when they released the studs in their new pastures last week. The only one that wasn't red faced was Maggie. Her countenance was as chilly as an icebox full of Budweiser on a hot summer's day.

"How big is your family," Emma asked, her cheeks rosy.

Sam could feel the smouldering fireworks going off between Emma and JJ. They couldn't keep their eyes off each other.

"My brother and sister live outside of Washington. Edwardo is a doctor and my sister has an accounting practice in the city. My brother-in-law is in the forces. He's overseas right now," JJ said, reaching for the plate of ham. "I opened a shop in New York after I finished my apprenticeship, Staten Island to be precise. It's a little gold mine."

"I went to New York to watch the Rodeo in Madison Square Gardens once," Mary offered. "That city scared the life out of me. It's so big."

"I love New York," Sylvie added, pointing a forkful of peas at Maggie. "We competed there a couple of times, didn't we, Mags?"

Maggie raised an eyebrow and played with the food on her plate.

Now Sam was really worried. Where was Maggie's explosion? Where were the sharp barbs? Heck, where were the fisticuffs? Zoe had just beaten her to the punch and had a ring to prove it!

There was a polite knock on the front door.

"I'll get it," BJ said, jumping out of his seat like a jack rabbit.

"Oh, New York is a wonderful place," JJ informed Mary. "You just need the right guide. Come stay with me and I'll show you around. I'll take you for a carriage ride in Grand Central Park or out to a show on Broadway."

"Now that's an offer I can't refuse," Mary giggled.

"I'll come with you," Emma jumped in.

"Go where," Cole said, striding into the kitchen.

Cole took one look at JJ and scowled. His face reddened as he stood towering over the good looking 'mechanic'.

Oh, the day was just getting better and better, Sam sighed.

"Who are you," Cole blurted out, one hand on his gun belt.

"Are you here to arrest me?" JJ joked, his eyes narrowing.

"Go find a chair, Cole," Sam ordered the sheriff. "You can pull up a seat between me and Sylvie."

"He still hasn't answered my question," Cole glowered, his normally placid face growing more rigid by the minute.

"Cole, go find a chair and sit," Emma commanded him. "This is JJ Cortez. He's Tommy's son. Zoe just got engaged to his father."

"Seriously," Cole guffawed.

"Hey, manners," JJ fumed. "My father's fiancée is sitting right over there."

"See," Zoe replied cheerfully, lifting her hand in the air. Zoe's hand had been fluttering back and forth like a butterfly all through dinner.

"Okay then," Cole stammered, heading off to the living room to find another chair.

"We're gonna need a bigger table," Sam mumbled under his breath.

"And a bottle of Jack Daniels," Sylvie whispered to him.

"That too," he agreed.

Sylvie's big belly laugh was infectious. Pretty soon, the tension around the table was broken and everyone except for Maggie laughed with her.

"What did I miss," Cole sulked as he returned with a fold up plastic chair.

"Zoe's engagement to a dirty-double-dealing-two-timing-cheating-scat," Maggie shouted, shoving away from the table. "And by the way, he asked me first, but I declined. How do you like my sloppy seconds?"

Oh, heck, Sam cursed. Here it comes!

Zoe leapt out of her seat, knocking her chair flying, and smashed a fist into Maggie's face. Luckily for Maggie, it wasn't the fist with the diamond. Maggie open handed Zoe across the face.

Zoe grabbed a handful of Maggie's hair and yanked hard. Maggie screamed and lifted Zoe off the floor, shaking her like a rag doll. More faces were slapped. Outside, the dogs went wild, barking up a storm.

Jenny screamed like a banshee, BJ looked about to faint, Mary cheered the fight on, Emma broke into tears, Sylvie started laughing uncontrollably, JJ and Cole battled against each other to try to break up the cat fight, and Sam sat at the head of the table stoically wishing he had let the bank foreclose on the ranch rather than taking in a bunch of crazy old women.

***

Sam sat on the porch in his favourite rocker smoking a pipe, Tommy's son in the chair beside him.

"My dad told me he loved them both," JJ sighed. "He said Maggie was more beautiful than words could describe and had a volcanic temper. My mother, God rest her soul, had a temper like that too. Papa always loved a challenge."

"Maggie is that," Sam agreed.

"I am so sorry for all of this," JJ apologized, lifting his gaze to meet Sam's.

"You've got nothing to be sorry for," Sam replied, tapping the ashes from his pipe into a clay ashtray. "Those two have been competing against each other since the first day they met."

Emma pushed open the front door, her face instantly blushing as her gaze fell upon JJ Cortez.

Sam would have chuckled except for the fact she was already dating Cole and Sam had had enough of love struck women for one night. Cole had left minutes ago and only because he got called out to a traffic accident.

"I was just apologizing to your father-in-law," JJ stammered, rising.

Sam hated to admit it, but he liked this young man, even if he was the son of a scoundrel.

"Oh, they'll sort it all out," Emma said, waving away JJ's apology. "They did before."

"But not until after a man was dead," Sam mumbled to himself.

Emma booted Sam's rocker.

"Things settled down upstairs?" he asked Emma.

"The dogs are comforting Jenny. Mary is in with Zoe. They are 'oohing' and 'ahhing' over the ring. Sylvie is dealing with Maggie in Maggie's room," Emma said, letting out a soft sigh of relief. "There isn't anymore screaming or hair pulling going on, if that is what you're asking?"

"That's good, I guess," Sam said, standing up. "Well, I'm gonna go help BJ with the barn chores."

JJ took that as a sign that it was time to go and stood up as well.

"Do you like horses, JJ," Emma queried the handsome man.

"I don't know," JJ smiled, the patio light making it look like there was a galaxy of stars shining brightly in each pupil. "I haven't been around them much, except for taking my mom on a couple of carriage rides before she passed."

"That's so sweet," Emma cooed.

Sam tipped his hat to JJ, cast Emma a warning look, and stepped down off the porch. The rain had cleared up. Time in the barn was just what he needed to put tonight's adventure behind him. Tomorrow was another day.

"Why don't you come by tomorrow and we'll go for a ride," Sam heard his daughter-in-law say to the convict's son.

This wasn't going to end well. Emma was a grown woman though. Her love life was none of his business unless it affected his grandkids.

Sam breathed in the cool evening air. Maybe it would rain tomorrow.

Chapter Nine

Boyfriends come and go, but horses are forever.

Mary climbed into bed, exhausted. She was the oldest of the ladies residing at *The Silver Spurs Home for Aging Cowgirls* at eighty-one. Even for her, there had been too much drama for one day; although, she had enjoyed the hair pulling event at dinner.

It had taken a half bottle of wine and a shot of dark rum in a cup of camomile tea to finally calm Zoe down enough to get her tucked into bed. The thought of assaulting the newly engaged woman had crossed Mary's mind as well. If Zoe flashed that ring in her face one more time, Mary refused to be responsible for her actions. At least, Mary reasoned, Zoe should sleep through the night and not escape to the stables in the middle of the night like she had done before. Sam's reversal of the front door locks from the outside to the inside had helped, but only when he remembered to lock up and remove the key from the keyhole.

The bedroom door squeaked open and Mary saw a giant furry face gazing at her hopefully from the doorway.

"Come on, Bulldozer," Mary said, patting the bed.

The giant Saint Bernard wagged her tail and leapt onto the end of the bed, settling down at Mary's feet. It was a good thing Mary was short.

"You too, Junior," Mary chuckled as Dozer Junior poked her nose through the door.

Junior galloped around the bed and dived onto it like it was a trampoline. Mary and Junior's mother bobbed up and down. The bed frame trembled with the combined weight of the two dogs and one human.

"Ohhh, you are such a good dog," Mary cooed, cupping her hands around the ninety pound puppy's massive face. Junior gave her a wet slobbery kiss. Mary grabbed the hand towel from the night table beside the bed and wiped the drool from her face. She was a sucker for dogs.

A soft tap-tap on the door followed suit.

"Come in," Mary said softly. "It's Grand Central Station in here tonight."

Sylvie crept into the bedroom, closing the door quietly behind her.

Mary turned on the night light before the room was plunged into darkness.

"Oh, my, that looks cozy," Sylvie giggled, blue eyes alive with mirth.

"If you can find an inch, you are welcome to it," Mary chortled, indicating the bed.

"That's okay, I won't stay long," Sylvie replied. "I need your help. I don't know what to do. This has gotten out of hand."

"I agree. It's worse than a family of racoons in the attic, arguing and humping above your head," Mary agreed.

Sylvie glanced at her oddly and then continued.

"Maggie is so stubborn. Can you believe Tommy asked her to be his pirate queen?" Sylvie declared with a shake of her red and silver locks. "She turned him down of course. Mags isn't a fool, despite her recent behaviour. She'd never marry a felon, especially one who is in there for life. She just doesn't like to lose. It's all ego."

"Yes, and Zoe can't stand being single," Mary agreed, tucking a pillow behind her back so she could sit up straighter. "At least Sam won't have to fill the boots of husband number seven. I'm sure he'll be glad about that."

"I know," Sylvie replied, amused. "We have to stop Zoe from making such a catastrophic mistake. It's not going to end well."

"But what can we do? She's a grown woman."

"I was hoping that you would come with me to the jail. Maybe we can talk some sense into Tommy?"

"I doubt that," Mary smirked. "That's a two carat diamond! If that doesn't scream 'I love you', 'I've got money to burn', 'I'm old and ugly and you don't seem to mind so marry me', nothing does."

Sylvie laughed lightly.

Dozer Junior woofed an objection.

The two women roared with laughter, and then covered their mouths to stop from waking everyone in the house.

"You're naughty," Sylvie blurted out.

"And you're naughtier," Mary snorted.

"So, will you come with me to the jail?"

"I will," Mary agreed. "Someone has to rescue that woman from herself, but what about Maggie?"

"If Mags could find a way to murder Tommy Cortez in his sleep, she would. I keep praying that one day she will change."

"We can always hope. We'll need an excuse to go see him," Mary murmured. "We can't have Maggie or Sam, for that matter, wanting to go with us. If we say we're going into town shopping, everyone will want to come. Although, Maggie and Zoe are so high maintenance maybe shopping will end their feud right then and there."

"Unless Zoe decides to go shop for a wedding dress," Sylvie mused. "I know, we'll tell everyone I have a follow up doctor's appointment and I asked you to drive me."

"Sam will want to take you if you tell him it's because of after effects from your stroke," Mary said.

"Point taken. How about I tell the old cowpoke it's a lady's issue? That'll stop him dead in his tracks."

The two women cackled again. They bumped fists. Sylvie kissed Bulldozer Senior on the forehead and slipped out of Mary's room.

Mary turned off her light and listened to Sylvie's light footsteps on the stairs as Sylvie returned to her room on the main floor of the ranch house.

Mary grinned and snuggled back down with the dogs. There was nothing like planning a secret mission to get the blood pumping.

***

Benny and Percy drove around the long term parking lot at the airport some two hours drive away from the penitentiary.

"I can't believe it? Where are all the cargo vans?" Benny hissed, driving past row after row of soccer mom vans and small cars.

"Maybe we need to find a warehouse district or something," Percy suggested, secretly happy that there weren't any cargo vans in sight.

"There's got to be one somewhere," Benny grumbled.

"Tell you what there is though. There's a whack of security cameras," Percy said, pointing at a camera mounted below a tall parking lot light.

Security cameras were affixed to every light standard. It was impossible to not be filmed breaking into a van given the lot was lit up like a Christmas tree.

"Yeah, mondo problemo," Benny agreed, his brows knitting together in frustration. "We'll circle back to the highway. I think I saw a bunch of industrial buildings close to the last gas station."

Percy watched a Boeing 746 land in the distance, its cabin lights blazing, and the heat from the engines visible even at this distance. The airport was bustling, despite the late hour.

The Bronco spun out of the parking lot as Benny followed the exit signs to the main highway. A soft mist hung in the air. Hard rock blared from the stereo. Benny banged his palms on the steering wheel in time with the drums. The lights from the dash board cast a greenish tint over his face.

Percy stared out the window at the passing cars and late night burger joints.

"There! There's one," Benny hollered, pointing towards a short squat cement building. The sign on the front of the building read: A-1 Industrial Cleaners. A navy blue and a white van were parked in front of the entrance doors. The navy blue van was rusted worse than the Bronco, the company's lettering almost completely worn off the side panel. The other van was shiny and new, the decals for A1 Industrial Cleaners bright and colourful.

"Let's see if that old beater runs," Benny suggested, pulling up beside the battered GMC cargo van.

Percy moaned, wanting nothing more than to hitch a ride to his mother's house. He hadn't seen her in two years, but she'd welcome him home. That's what mom's did, right?

Benny parked the Bronco and rifled behind the seat for a slim-jim and a pair of pliers. He exited the Bronco and slipped the slim-jim down the window, fishing around until he was able to pop the lock.

"Can you frigging believe it," Benny shouted, a set of spare keys falling onto the seat as his head bumped the visor.

"No, I can't," Percy stuttered, getting out of the Bronco. Lady Luck was not with him tonight.

Benny placed the ignition key in the lock and turned it. The GMC coughed into life.

"Geez, there's even a half full tank of gas," his friend laughed.

"You want me to follow you in the Bronco," Percy asked hopefully.

"Nope, hop in," Benny said, leaving the blue van running. "I got a billy can of gas in the Bronco so we don't have to gas up. We'll park the van at the truck stop just past the penitentiary. Dad thinks the ladies will visit in the next couple of days. They got a wedding to plan. Can you believe one of those dames actually agreed to marry that hoser? Anyway, we got to watch for a big white dually with a horse trailer hitch in the back bed. There can't be too many old broads driving duallys around. Am I right or am I right?"

Percy nodded, his intestines twisting into knots as he slipped behind the wheel of the soon to be stolen panel van. This all sounded great in the bar; now, maybe not so much. Lord knows, he could use the money. He planned on opening a gym with it. Yeah, that would be cool… his own gym.

Benny closed the driver's door and jogged back to the Bronco. He started it up and drove away.

Percy pulled out of A-1 Industrial Supplies wondering if the guy who'd been driving the van would still have a job in the morning. He felt bad for the guy, but hey, leaving a set of keys above the visor and then just locking a vehicle up? What a bozo.

Oh, well, he shrugged, not his problem.

Percy turned the dial on the radio to FM 73.5 country. Charlie Daniel's *The Devil Went Down to Georgia* crackled over the van's speakers. Percy smiled. He loved that song.

"Johnny, rosin up your bow and play your fiddle hard... 'Cause Hell's broke loose in Georgia, and the devil deals the cards. And if you win, you get this shiny fiddle made of gold, but if you lose, the devil gets your soul...," Percy belted out, not realizing the irony of the lyrics.

Chapter Ten

A polo pony is like a motorbike with a mind of its own weighing half a ton.

Emma hummed along to Miranda Lambert's *Bluebird* as she whipped up a dozen eggs for breakfast. The tantalizing smell of bacon filled the air as it sizzled on racks in the oven.

She had already talked to JJ. He would swing by the ranch after lunch. She was playing with fire. Cole would be furious when he found out she went riding with JJ, but he would get over it. Cole had been hinting for awhile now, testing her to see if she was ready to make a full commitment. Cole hadn't asked her to marry him...yet.

So why was she doing this, she asked herself. *Rebellion? Fear of commitment?*

JJ reminded her of Gus Rodriquez. She had her chance with Gus, but had decided Cole was the better choice, and then Gus had fallen for her friend, Dee. After losing her husband in Iraq, Emma had sworn never to date anyone with a career that put them in jeopardy. Gus was an ATF agent. He dealt with the most brutal of criminals. Cole handed out speeding tickets and broke up bar fights on a Saturday night. They were different, right?

Truth was, she didn't know why she was avoiding Cole all of a sudden.

Was she still in love with her late husband Cleve? Yes.

Did she want to fall in love again? Yes. She was lonely, mind numbingly so. The cold emptiness on the other side of the bed at night ate her up, mind, body and soul.

What was the problem then? Ugh, she didn't know.

Cole was sweet, handsome and devoted to her and the kids. Plain and simple, Cole Trane was a good man.

JJ Cortez was drop dead gorgeous with a winning smile and a delightfully wicked sense of humour. His job didn't put him in jeopardy every day either. He had good manners too. She wouldn't have expected that from a drug king pin's son, but what did she know?

Maybe it was hanging around the four crazy old women who lived with her? Their antics and joie de vivre were wearing off on her.

Emma smiled at the thought of the four grandma cowgirls, as Jenny referred to them, willing to take a chance on pretty much anything.

"You are far too chipper this morning," Sylvie grumbled, strolling into the kitchen, a white terry bathrobe pulled over her pink flannel pjs. Sylvie poured herself a cup of coffee and sat down at the table.

"That's because a certain swarthy young man is paying a visit," Mary chirped as she entered the kitchen dressed in jeans and a colourful Navaho print sweater.

"Look at you, you're all dressed up with nowhere to go," Sylvie joked.

"I thought I'd go for a ride this morning," Mary grinned, fixing herself a cup of tea. "It takes work to keep this shapely figure of mine. You never know when some handsome fella is going to ask me to marry him."

"That's true, you never know," Emma agreed, her eyes twinkling with mirth. Mary Adams was a real catch in her day and had dodged getting hitched many times. She bragged about it regularly.

"Morning ladies," Sam's baritone voice rumbled like thunder through the kitchen as he made his way to the coffee pot.

"Jenny make it to the school bus on time?" Sam asked Emma.

"She did," Emma replied, placing a couple of slices of bread in the toaster. "I expect she'll sleep all the way to school."

"Yeah, that was a bit of a hum-dinger yesterday," Sylvie mumbled, eyeing Sam over top of her coffee cup.

"More like a category five if you ask me," Sam grinned as he sat down at the head of the table, coffee mug in hand. "I'm thinking we better split those two up from now on. Might make for quieter suppers."

"Party pooper," Mary quipped.

Sam raised an eyebrow and glanced at Mary disapprovingly. Mary smirked back. She had known Sam Montana a long time.

"So what are your plans today," Sam queried Sylvie.

"I have a doctor's appointment this afternoon," Sylvie lied smoothly.

"What time? I have to go pick up some fencing supplies. I can take you," Sam offered as Emma took the tray of bacon out of the oven.

"That's okay Sam, I'll take Sylvie," Mary jumped in.

"It's a ladies thing," Sylvie leaned over and whispered into Sam's ear.

Sam blushed.

"Alright then," he scowled into his coffee.

Emma noticed Mary and Sylvie glance conspiratorially at each other as she set a tray of bacon and toast on the table while the eggs finished cooking in the skillet on the stove. Something was up.

Zoe stumbled into the room, her eyes red rimmed, a mild black and blue bruise on her right cheek.

"Would you like a steak to put on that shiner," Sam asked the grey-faced woman.

"No, I'm fine, thank you," Zoe replied demurely.

"Why don't you sit beside me for a change," Sam said, pulling out the chair on the far side of him.

"That's okay," the hung over woman mumbled. "I'm just going to grab a tea and a piece of toast and head back to my room."

"A little under the weather, are we?" Sylvie smiled crookedly.

"Hmmm, just a tad," Zoe confessed.

"You go ahead and help yourself to toast and jam," Emma nodded, sliding a side plate across the table. "And you all leave Mrs. Puddicombe be."

"Yes, mom," Sam teased his daughter-in-law.

Emma glared back.

"So, Cole know you're taking JJ out for a spin this afternoon," Sam kidded as he helped himself to a slice of bacon.

"If you aren't careful, you're going to end up with a shiner," Emma informed the cheeky old man smiling up at her.

"See? That's why I love living here," Mary beamed. "You never know what's going to happen next."

Maggie chose that moment to make her entrance. She wore a flowing black silk nightgown with a red sash tied around the waist, her luxurious mane of hair falling in a dark pool around her shoulders, looking none the worse for wear.

Zoe, holding a plate of toast and cup of tea tightly against her breast, lifted her chin and strode past the angular faced woman, continuing out the kitchen and up the stairs without a word.

Maggie let out a disgruntled sigh and sat down at the table, flicking her hair back like an irate school girl.

"Will you be eating breakfast with us this morning, Maggie," Emma asked casually.

"Of course," was Maggie's terse reply.

Emma placed a dinner plate on the table in front of her most difficult tenant.

"I'm going for a ride this morning," Mary offered. "Anyone care to join me? What about you, Maggie?"

"No, thank you," Maggie said, fingering her cutlery.

"Oh, come on, Mags. Let's all go," Sylvie replied cheerily. "It will be fun, three old broads on three equally old stallions, out on the trails, enjoying the air. We can wear those new cowboy hats we bought a few months ago. They aren't just for poker night, you know?"

Maggie laughed despite her ill temper.

Emma was glad to hear it.

"Absolutely," Mary grinned. "I can't wait to see that stallion of yours buck you off at the first butterfly that crosses his path."

There was silence at the table.

"You're right, Mary, perhaps I should wear a hard hat instead of a cowboy hat," Maggie agreed.

A gale of laughter broke out around the table as Emma passed around the rest of the plates.

***

Emma saw JJ wave to Mary and Sylvie from his rental car as the ladies passed him in Mary's truck on the way out the drive. A thick cloud of blue black smoke billowed out of the tail pipe of Mary's battered old Ford dually pickup truck. Maybe when they got back from Sylvie's appointment, JJ could have a look at Mary's truck. It sounded like the big diesel hadn't had a tune up in years. It was amazing the Ford was still on the road.

Emma finished saddling up BJ's buckskin. Penny, Emma's smaller bay Quarter horse was already saddled. She figured she'd ride Bucky and let JJ ride Penny given that Penny was the quieter of the two.

She waved and smiled at JJ as he slowly pulled up in front of the two story sage green coloured barn. Emma's peach coloured hair framed her round freckled face. Her heart skipped a beat and her cheeks burned.

"Show no fear," she said to herself as the athletic swarthy mechanic climbed out of the car.

"Hi," he said, walking towards her.

"Back at you," Emma smiled.

"Umm, which one is mine," JJ asked, casting a worried glance at Bucky. Bucky was a good six inches taller than Penny at the withers. "The shorter one, I hope."

"Yes, you'll be riding Penny. She's my horse. She'll look after you," Emma chuckled, nodding towards the bay.

JJ grinned as he approached the horses. He tentatively reached out to pat Penny on the neck. The mare sighed with pleasure. Penny was a real love bug and not the usual temperamental type of mare.

"I think she likes me," JJ beamed.

So far, so good, Emma thought, pleased, despite the butterflies in her stomach. She felt a little bit like she was cheating on Cole, but was she really? Cole and she weren't engaged, they were just dating. Emma was simply being a hospitable host, wasn't she? After all, JJ's father was engaged to one of her tenants.

"Okay, let's do this," JJ said, letting out a breath.

She met his steady gaze with her own, his broad face and earnest look quickening her pulse. She felt like a kid on her first day at a new school.

"Right," Emma stammered, unclipping Penny's halter and slipping on the bridle, "a few basics first."

"Yes, ma'am," JJ grinned, and saluted her.

Emma giggled.

"You always mount a horse from the left side."

"Why?"

"In the old days, a right-handed man carried his sword on his left side. He mounted on the left so the sword wouldn't get in the way as he swung up into the saddle," Emma replied.

"That makes sense, but I didn't bring my sword, or my armour," JJ joked. "Oh wait, I'm left handed so that means I should mount on the other side."

"I wouldn't recommend it," Emma continued, exasperated. "Horses see different from us. They see sideways instead of straight ahead so everything looks different from one side to the other. Penny is okay because I trained her to allow me to mount on either side, but some horses will buck you off if you mount them from the right."

"I had no idea," JJ blurted out, his eyes widening. "I guess it's a good thing I have such a beautiful and experienced teacher for my first ride on the range."

Oh, boy, Emma smirked. They hadn't even left the yard and she was already in trouble.

"Stop it," she ordered him.

"Stop what?"

"You're making me get flustered," Emma scolded him lightly.

"Is that such a bad thing," he winked.

JJ slipped the reins out of Emma's hands, casually brushing her fingertips with his as he did so. He clucked to

Penny, backing her up easily, flipped the reins over the mare's head, placed a foot in the stirrup and slid into the saddle like a pro. He moved the mare off his leg by applying gentle pressure to one side and then the other, casually checking her responsiveness, all while holding the reins lightly in one hand.

"I thought you said you'd never ridden before," Emma hissed, wagging a warning finger at him.

"I may have misspoken. I may have ridden a little bit when I was a kid," JJ confessed, his eyes twinkling with mirth.

"A little bit, huh! Well, that's not very knightly of you," Emma answered, frustrated.

"Maybe I just wanted to watch you mount that big horse," he said, quickly backing the mare out of Emma's reach.

"Oh, you... you....," Emma grumbled, taking hold of Bucky's reins and then the saddle horn. She hauled herself up into the saddle. She wasn't quite as agile mounting the tall buckskin as she was her little mare.

"I was going to bring you flowers, but I didn't know if you preferred your roses with or without thorns," JJ chortled.

"Ooooh, you are cheeky, aren't you," she griped, unable to stay mad. He was so darned charming.

"My lady," the gorgeous hunk chimed, bowing in acquiescence. "Seriously, thorns or no thorns, smelly or not smelly? I need to know."

Yep, Emma laughed, she was in way over her head with JJ Cortez.

Chapter Eleven

My horse is security conscious… he always likes to bolt
the stable door when I leave.

"Mary, slow down," Sylvie gasped as she caught a glimpse of an inmate in the yard who looked strikingly similar to her late husband. He had the same jaunty step, middle aged paunch, and balding head with a grey pony tail folded over his collar.

"I swear that's Cade!"

"But Cade is dead," Mary scowled, slowing down so Sylvie could get a better view of the inmates in the yard.

"I know. I killed him," Sylvie stammered. "There's no way he survived strangulation, not once but twice, and a fall from a second story window!"

"Then it can't be Cade, can it?" Mary reasoned.

The orange clad inmates in the yard strolled about. Some played basketball while others just walked in circles well back from the electric security fence. Most, however, sat in the bleachers enjoying the fresh air. There were only three inmates wearing red coveralls.

"I think that's Tommy, over there," Sylvie pointed.

"Definitely looks like him" Mary agreed. "Short, dark and wrinkly."

Sylvie chuckled.

"You're right," Sylvie agreed, turning around. "I must be getting dotty. That can't be Cade."

"Don't lose it now," Mary moaned. "We got us a bandit to convince to dump his fiancée. That won't be easy."

"I'm still working out how we can get him to do that," Sylvie confessed.

Mary rolled her eyes as she drove into the parking lot.

***

The rusted Ford pulled into the parking lot in front of the prison. There were a lot of visitors today so the truck circled the lot a couple of times before the driver settled on a parking spot in the shade of an oak tree whose leaves had just begun to unfold at the back of the lot.

"That must be them," Benny said, smacking Percy awake. "Big dually. Fifth wheel hook in the bed. Two old women."

"Are you sure?" Percy asked from the passenger seat of the white Bronco. He looked over at the driver, a tiny white haired cowgirl in a rustic suede coat, jeans and cowboy boots, and her companion, a long red and silver haired woman in designer jeans, ankle boots and tailored woollen jacket, as they stepped out of the truck and walked side by side across the parking lot towards the entry gate.

"They don't look that pretty to me. I thought you said they were real stunning. I mean, not that they aren't okay for their age, but you said one of them looked like Cher," Percy continued.

"Yeah, well, my dad's never seen them up close," Benny growled. "He just knows one of them drives a dually, the other a Beamer, and they're old as the hills."

"But these two came together and they're going into the prison together as well," Percy whined. "What if they're the wrong women?"

"They aren't," Benny seethed. "I'll follow them in to make sure they're going to see Cortez. Will that make you feel better?"

"Yeah," Percy nodded.

"When I come back, we'll go get the van," Benny snarled, slamming the door behind him. "We'll just have to settle for a two'fer instead of one at a time."

"This is all wrong, bro," Percy mumbled to himself.

***

Mary and Sylvie entered the prison.

"I've never been to prison before," Mary whispered, her eyes widening as she saw all the guards checking visitor's bags and identification.

"Me neither," Sylvie whispered back. "Act normal and don't talk back."

"Talk back? Me? It's you that needs to mind your manners," Mary quipped. "You are a self-confessed murderer after all."

"Shhhh," Sylvie hushed her friend as they waited in line.

Sylvie sensed a dark presence behind her. She shivered, expecting to see the Boogieman or that Jason character, maybe even Freddie Krueger, behind her. Instead, there was a jittery kid with a weird punk rock hairstyle. The blond spikes and brown hair shorn like a Marine at the sides almost made her laugh. She turned back around, her stomach in knots.

"Who are you here to see," the guard at the scanner table asked.

"Tommy Cortez," Mary piped up.

Sylvie caught a flicker of motion off to one side and looked back in time to see the spike haired punk exiting the building. Huh, she thought, that was strange.

"Tommy?" the guard smirked. "Jeez, that guy has more lady visitors than anyone else in the joint. I don't get it."

"We haven't seen you before," another guard said, stepping forward with an air of authority. He looked the two women over.

"We're friends of Zoe, his fiancée," Sylvie jumped in. "We need to talk to him about the upcoming nuptials."

"We weren't exactly sure what to expect," Mary added, her eyes and smile dazzlingly bright. "It's not every day we get to plan a prison wedding. Will you be coming? Should we be inviting everyone? That's an awful lot of men to cook for."

"No, ma'am, you don't have to invite the whole prison and as for the guards, it will depend on who is on shift," the senior guard laughed. "We do have a nice chapel though and a pastor that comes in three days a week."

"Well, you just give me a list of guards who will be there and I'll make sure I personally write out the invitations," Mary beamed.

"Miss Adams, Miss O'Hara," the lead guard grinned, handing back their ID. "Place your purses on the belt. I'll have a guard bring Tommy in from the yard. He's a lucky man to have such a fine group of ladies looking after him."

"Yes, he is," Mary grinned back, placing her hand bag on the belt, "and please call me Mary. So, tell me, er… sorry, I didn't get your name."

"Art, ma'am," the senior guard replied.

"Tell me, Art, are you single," Mary winked as she sashayed through the scanner. "Not for me, mind you, I'm a happy spinster, but you never know when I might meet a suitable young lady looking for a big handsome employed male to settle down with."

So much for being discreet, Sylvie mused.

The guards howled with laughter.

"I am," the younger guard behind the scanner raised his hand.

"Oh, that's so sweet, but you're far too young to get married," Mary admonished the young man. "You need to have fun. Go dancing, drink and be merry."

"This way, Miss Adams," Art laughed heartily, leading the way.

Sylvie hooked arms with Mary. Mary sparkled. Sylvie tried not to giggle as they skipped along the hallway trying to keep up with the long legged guard named Art in front of them. Sylvie knew how Alice felt when she fell down the rabbit hole. The prison was a whole different world.

***

Percy propped open the hood of the GMC van so that it looked like he was having engine trouble. Benny laid waiting in the rear of the van with duck tape and ropes. He had a handgun in case the ladies put up a fight. That hadn't sounded right to Percy. How much fight could two seniors put up?

Percy bit his lip, a frown creasing his forehead. This wasn't anything like they had planned. They were supposed to kidnap the women one at a time and there had been no mention of guns.

Benny had assured him that the old broads would stop if he flagged them down. The ladies were from a time when you stopped to help a stranger out, or so Benny had said. Percy wasn't as convinced.

Percy heard a series of loud thumps coming from the inside of the van. Benny must have seen them coming through the rear windows.

The handsome blond-haired blue-eyed Adonis put on his best smile as he walked around the side of the van lifting one hand in the air and waving to the occupants of the weathered dually truck coming towards him on the dusty side road between the highway and the penitentiary.

***

"That man is infuriating," Sylvie seethed. "Can you believe that arrogant so-and-so?"

"He was a drug lord, remember," Mary replied, squinting into the sun.

"He's a wolf in a demi-god's clothing," Sylvie spat.

"I think you mean 'sheep's clothing'," Mary nodded.

"That would be doing the sheep a disservice."

"What did you expect?" Mary asked. "He's had two women fawning over him for months, stroking his ego, and now he's conned one of them into marrying him. He's as puffed up as a blow fish. They're poisonous, you know? Blow fish, I mean."

"I know," Sylvie scowled. "I'm just so darned mad."

Mary drove on.

"Oh, dear, look," Mary said, nodding towards the man on the side of the road trying to flag them down. "That nice young boy looks like he needs our help."

"Keep driving," Sylvie growled. "We're the ones that need help."

"I can't do that, it wouldn't be right," Mary quipped, pulling up beside Percy. "Roll down your window, Sylvie."

"Thanks for stopping," Percy gushed, leaning through the passenger side window and flashing a perfect smile.

It was so bright, the sun darned near glinted off his teeth, Sylvie noticed.

"I stopped to answer my phone and my van died, and then when I went to call for a tow truck, my phone died."

"You're batting a thousand, aren't you?" Mary grinned.

"I have jumper cables," Percy said. "Do you think you could give me a jump?"

"No, but we'll call someone for you," Sylvie snickered, fishing in her purse for her cell phone.

"Of course we'll help," Mary smirked. "Don't mind my friend; she's had a bad awakening."

"Oh, that's awesome," Percy replied. "If you pull around the front of the van, I'll grab my cables."

Sylvie rolled up her window as Mary manoeuvred the Ford in line with the van. Mary popped the hood open. The giant hood blocked their view of the van itself. The truck's doors were yanked open at the same time.

Sylvie was hauled out of the truck and dragged scratching and kicking to the side door of the GMC van. She cursed and tried to bite her attacker, the wired punk-haired freak from the prison lobby, but only succeeded in gagging on the rag he stuffed down her throat. Her instincts had told her there was something wrong and now here she was being tossed none too gently into the van. To make things worse, the punk rocker started wrapping her arms and legs with duck tape.

The steroid kid beside her was doing the same to Mary. At least, if she was going to be kidnapped, she wasn't alone. If only Mary would have listened to her!

Chapter Twelve

*There's no shame in fear. But understand this — the coward is
ruled by fear, while the hero rides it like a wild stallion.*
David Gemmell, *Fear, Hero, Coward*

It was a long and bumpy ride from the prison to where
ever the two men were taking them. The gravel crunching
beneath the wheels meant it was somewhere remote. That
didn't bode well.

Sylvie couldn't figure out why she and Mary were being
kidnapped. The kidnappers were sadly mistaken if they
thought she was worth a lot of money. Mary was a no
brainer: look at the truck she drove?

Sylvie had netted a cool one and a half million from the
sale of her equestrian property. Between the interest
earned and the funds themselves, it meant she was good to
reside at the Montana's ranch for the rest of her life
provided she didn't get thrown into prison first. Sylvie had
privately changed her Will. Upon death, the Montana
family got it all. She wanted to make sure that her stallion
had a home until his end of days and BJ and Jenny had a

chance to go to college or university if they wanted. There was no way Sylvie was going to give the bozos that kidnapped her one single penny.

The van groaned, its springs wailing as it sunk deep into a series of potholes. She bounced into the air, slamming down against the van's rear wheel well with spine numbing force. She would have yelped, but the soggy gag in her mouth prevented it.

She reached out with her feet, scooting her bum around ninety degrees until she was able to tap Mary on the leg with her boots. Mary didn't respond. The potato sack the kidnappers had thrown over Sylvie's head prevented her from seeing her compatriot. She suspected Mary had a sack over her head too.

After what felt like hours, the rickety contractor's van ground to a stop.

She heard the front doors open and then close. The side door scraped open. A cold wind blew through the opening. It chilled her to the bone. They must be somewhere in the mountains.

"Grab that one first, she kicks the hardest," the punk rocker snarled.

Just to be ornery, Sylvie kicked out, her boot soles connecting with the stomach of whichever of the boys grabbed her. She grinned inwardly when she heard a loud 'oomph'.

"Bitch," the punk rocker spat, flipping her over and dragging her by the arms backwards out of the van.

"There's something wrong with this one," the steroid Adonis stuttered. "She's not breathing."

"She's faking it," the punk rocker argued. "Haul her out of there and get her inside."

"But…"

"Do it," Adonis's partner shouted.

Fear caught in Sylvie's throat.

Was the blond haired steroid kidnapper she thought of as Adonis right? Was Mary dead?

The retired barrel racer was in her eighties. Perhaps her heart had given out?

If they killed Jenny's cowgirl grandma, there would be Hell to pay, and not just at Sylvie's hands either!

The moron with the spiked hair dragged her across the hard packed ground. Pain tore through her shoulders, wrists and back. If the idiot had untied the duck tape from her legs she could have walked. She also could have kicked him in the nuts. Guess he knew that.

A door squeaked open.

The smell of decay and dust assailed her senses as she was hauled into some kind of a building. The smell hung in the air with a cloying heaviness that made it even harder to breathe. Sweat dripped down her face causing the burlap bag over her head to stick to her hair and cheeks. It was both claustrophobic and itchy.

Footsteps echoed in the hall behind her.

Her tail bone cracked as her butt hit the floor. A wave of dizziness passed over her. She felt rather than heard Mary being placed on the floor beside her.

A rope was slipped over her shoulders, its ends cutting into her waist as it was tightened far more than it needed to be. She was hauled backwards into a sitting position.

She felt something hard against her spine and realized it was a wall and not open air.

"I'm taking the bag off her," the Adonis quaked, his voice dripping with worry. "I don't care what you say. She isn't breathing."

Sylvie heard a rustle and felt the jostle of Mary's body against her right hip and thigh.

"Your funeral," the punk rocker quipped.

If she wasn't so woozy, she would have held her breath. She wished she could see what was happening.

"Come on, lady," Adonis murmured. "Breathe!"

Mary's body began to shake. It trembled, her friend's legs rubbing back and forth along the length of Sylvie's own.

What were they doing to her friend?

Rage replaced the worry inside Sylvie's breast. She wanted to rip these boys' heads off, maybe shove a set of panties down their mouths and watch them gag. She did it once, she could do it again. With a start, she realized they had pretty much done that to her?

God, please tell me I don't have men's tightie-whities in my mouth, she prayed.

"What the heck are you doing to her," the punk rocker yelled.

"CPR," Adonis gasped, his breathing coming short and swift as he pumped air into Mary's chest.

Suddenly, Sylvie heard a sharp intake of breath.

"Breeeatheeee," Adonis's soft voice crooned. "You can do it."

Good for the steroid brat, maybe there was hope after all?

Relief flooded through Sylvie when she heard a guttural moan. Now if only that muscle bound idiot would remove Sylvie's potato sack from over her head and take the rag out of her mouth as well.

"There, you happy, she's alive," the punk rocker sneered.

"Yeah, I'll give her some water when she wakes up," Adonis sighed with relief.

"I'm out'a here. I'm gonna ditch the van. I'll be back later with some grub for you and the dames. Tomorrow, I'll signal my dad to deliver the ransom note. Wish I could see that old bandit's face when he finds out we got his women. Hah!"

'Old bandit'? 'His women'? Were they talking about Tommy Cortez? Did they think they had taken Zoe and Maggie?

Sylvie winced. The bumbling fools kidnapped the wrong gals. This wasn't good. She had to let Mary know, but how?

***

"Where are Sylvie and Mary?" Maggie asked, sitting down at the kitchen table.

"They haven't come back from town yet?" Sam grumbled as he took the seat beside Maggie.

"That's odd," Zoe said, sweeping into the room, still in her nightgown from that morning. The bruise on her cheek was now a deep shade of purple with a hint of blue at the edges.

110

"And they didn't call?" Maggie inquired, pursing her lips. "That isn't like Sylvie."

"I assume they decided to have supper in town," Emma replied, her face pinched.

Sam could see his daughter-in-law was angry but trying not to show it.

"Mary isn't like that either, she would call," Zoe insisted, pouring herself a glass of water from the pitcher on the table. "Did they take Mary's truck? Maybe it's broken down on the road somewhere?"

Zoe was right, Sam simmered. Mary would phone if there was an issue, and so would Sylvie. Well, it was only five o'clock. Maybe the doctor's appointment ran late? Maybe they decided to go shopping after the appointment? There was a lot of 'maybes'. Women!

Jenny burst into the house in a flurry of excitement.

"I got him running," she hollered, her exuberance bubbling over.

"More like a fast walk," BJ laughed as he followed his sister into the kitchen.

"That's great, baby, how far did you go today," Emma asked her daughter.

"We ran a whole mile, didn't we BJ," Jenny grinned, rushing to the sink to wash her hands.

"Close to it, I guess," BJ agreed, waiting for his sister to finish up.

"Mike was awesome," Jenny giggled, drying her hands on a kitchen towel. "I think he's happy, happy, happy."

"No he's not," BJ mumbled, sticking his dirty hands under the water. "Dozer and Junior had fun though."

111

Sam couldn't help but smile. His granddaughter was determined, he'd give her that. The jury was out on whether Mike would actually make it to race day without going lame, but so far the fifty year-old donkey had surprised him and was hanging in there.

"Where's Miss Sylvie and Mary," Jenny queried, her face beaming as she plunked her bottom down on a wood spindled chair.

"They haven't got back from town yet," Emma answered, placing a bowl of beef stew on the table in front of Jenny. "I'm sure they'll be along soon."

"Awww, I wanted to tell them how great Mike was," Jenny whined.

"BJ, before you sit, feed the dogs," Emma told her son.

"Yes, mum," BJ nodded, drying his hands. He stepped around her and went to the pantry cupboard where they kept a garbage bin stuffed to the brim with Purina Dog Chow.

"And put a cupful of stew on top of their kibble," Emma added, depositing large bowls of stew in front of her paying guests.

"In my day, we only fed the dogs people food," Maggie announced unexpectedly. "The store bought food was horrendous."

"You had a dog, Maggie," Jenny gasped in surprise.

"Dogs, as in plural," Maggie smiled. "I had four in fact. They were Corgis, just like the Queen of England has. They were marvellous dogs."

"How come you don't have any now," Emma inquired, as surprised as everyone else around the table.

"It's too hard to say goodbye," Maggie whispered sadly.

Maggie Carroll was a conundrum, Sam mused, eyeing the woman thoughtfully. Most of the time, he couldn't stand her, and then she'd come up with something so deeply personal he wondered if he maybe he was being too hard on her.

BJ left to feed the dogs while everyone dug into their dinner.

"So, how did your ride go this afternoon," Zoe asked, after BJ returned to the table.

"It was fun," Emma blushed.

"How fun," Maggie asked, raising an eyebrow, the corners of her mouth twitching. "Uneventful fun or over the moon fun?"

"Yes, do tell?" Sam chortled.

Emma's face reddened even more.

"Well, it seems that JJ was holding back," Emma smirked. "He is a very good rider. He had a pony when he was growing up. Apparently, he even won some ribbons at a horse show."

"Why am I not surprised?" Zoe laughed.

"Did he ride barrels," Jenny asked. "I bet he did."

"He was a jumper, he said, but he got too haughty after he won some prestigious show so his mother sent him to cowboy camp to teach him a lesson. JJ said it didn't go as planned; he loved it. When he found out how much the vaqueros got paid, he gave up horses, and went to school to become a mechanic," Emma informed her rapt audience.

"That's cool," BJ nodded, digging his spoon deep into the bowl of stew. "Maybe he can help during branding season?"

Sam remained mute. He liked Tommy's son well enough but didn't fancy having him hanging around his grandkids or his daughter-in-law. There was also the question of Sheriff Cole Trane. Sam wasn't sure Emma had thought things through very well. She and Cole had been an item for months and friends since childhood. Cole didn't know about the trail ride...yet!

"After dinner, we'll bring in the horses, BJ," Sam said. "There's another storm coming in."

"I can help," Jenny offered hopefully.

"Don't you have homework to do?" he replied.

"Yeah, but not a lot," the little girl answered sheepishly.

"Do your home work," Emma commanded. "The boys can look after the horses. BJ, you do yours after you bring those studs in as well."

"Yes, mom," he grinned, wiping up the last of his stew with a homemade dinner roll.

"I'll give Sylvie a buzz on her cell after dinner," Maggie offered. "If she doesn't pick up or call back, I'll drive into town to see if I can find her."

"Not alone, you won't," Sam grumbled.

"I'll go too," Zoe insisted. "They're my friends also."

Maggie glared across the table at the woman she gave the shiner to.

Sam expected fireworks again, but apparently the two women had done a little growing up since last night.

"Emma, I'll take the cell with me if we go," Sam replied stiffly, pushing away from the table. "If the gals come home or call, phone me."

"You think I should call Cole?" Emma responded, her face reflecting his concern.

"Not yet," Sam growled. "We'll give it another hour or so before we go charging off like a herd of stampeding ponies."

Sam stomped out of the house.

"You're really worried, aren't you, grandpa," BJ huffed, jogging along beside him.

"I am, but I don't want to scare the ladies or your mother or sister," Sam agreed.

"Thought so," BJ confirmed. "It isn't like Miss Sylvie or Miss Mary not to call like that."

"Nope, it's not."

Sam bit his lip. If he could get a minute alone, he'd call Cole himself.

All afternoon, he'd had a feeling that Mary and Sylvie had been up to something. The doctor's office was long closed, but maybe Cole could confirm if Sylvie even had a doctor's appointment at all. Cole would have the doctor's emergency number.

Sylvie was a slippery one. He wouldn't put it past her to lie to him if she was about to do something she knew he wouldn't approve of, but Mary was a different story. What could the two women be involved in that neither of them wanted him to know about? Whatever it was, it made the hair go up on the back of his neck. His instincts told him, it had gotten them into trouble!

Chapter Thirteen

A horse gallops with his lungs, perseveres with his heart, and wins with his character.
Tesio

Sylvie shivered. Her hands and feet numb from both the cold and the duck tape wrapped around them. Finally, her blond haired and blue eyed abductor had removed the burlap sack from over her head and taken the filthy rag out of her mouth. The musty air was ambrosia to her lungs.

She gratefully accepted the water he poured gently into her mouth.

"Why on earth are you doing this?" Mary asked, her voice warbling like an out of tune piano.

Sylvie glared at her, shaking her head perceptibly. She hoped Mary would get it. Adonis didn't know he had the wrong victims. Her friend stared back, a blank expression on her face.

"What?" Mary grumbled.

"What my friend means to ask is how much do you think Tommy is willing to pay to get his fiancée and mistress back?"

Sylvie saw Mary's eyes widened in surprise. They looked as round as a Disney cartoon character. Now, she got it. Praise the Lord, Sylvie grinned.

"How did you figure it out?" the young man gaped.

"I didn't until now," Sylvie smiled, hoping the young man wouldn't shut down on her. She was pretty sure he had a conscience. He had performed CPR on Mary. "I have money, but not enough to kidnap me for. My beloved now, he's loaded."

"So you're his fiancée then," the Adonis grinned back, a smug look of satisfaction on his face.

"Yes, she most certainly is," Mary exclaimed with a wink at Sylvie.

Sylvie groaned.

How obvious could Mary be?

"You do know who Tommy is, don't you?" Sylvie continued. "You and your partner don't actually think he'll let you get away with this?"

"He won't you know," Mary replied gleefully. "He'll call his goons in. I wouldn't want to be in your shoes then, young fella. Tommy can be cruel. I mean, have you seen his face. He didn't get ugly like that by being an angel."

Sylvie rolled her eyes. If Mary continued, she was going to get them killed.

"Again, what my friend, Maggie, here is saying is that if you let us go, I will make sure that Tommy pays you a substantial finder's fee," Sylvie replied.

"A really substantial finder's fee," Mary echoed.

"And you won't get killed while waiting for the ransom to be delivered or spend the rest of your days running for your life," Sylvie said, risking a wink at the not-so-bright gym fanatic leaning over her with a bottle of water in one hand and a Snicker's bar in the other.

"I'd never turn on Benny," he barked.

He stood up and flexed his muscles.

Sylvie had to admit, he was a handsome bloke. Too bad he was so dumb; still the seeds of doubt were planted.

Sylvie smirked. Mary grinned back. That was all Sylvie had planned for the moment.

"I don't suppose you have a blanket do you?" Mary asked lightly. "It's awfully cold in here and I'm old enough to be your grandmother. My fingers and toes feel like they've been donated to Captain Highliner. You wouldn't do that to your granny, would you, serve up her appendages with French fries?"

"I don't have a granny," Adonis sulked, "and that makes no sense whatsoever."

"Oh, that's so sad," Mary commiserated.

The kidnapper disappeared into the shadowy room on the other side of where they were seated. He returned with a couple of sleeping bags and a camp lantern. He tossed the sleeping backs over top of them and then lit the lantern. The light chased away the creeping shadows. The warm glow instantly provided some marginal relief from the cold.

Sylvie noted that they were in a very old building, obviously long since abandoned. Fluttery bits of cobwebs hung in the corners, but most had been swept away. There were long thin slits in the weathered boards along the wall where the mud insulation had crumbled and disintegrated. Beside her was a rusted iron stove; the rope circling hers and Mary's waists was tied to it.

It must be around six o'clock, she thought, given the shortness of daylight filtering through the windows in the far room. Emma and Sam would be wondering where they were. She hoped they wouldn't make the news. If one of the kidnappers saw it, they would know they had the wrong women. She didn't think Adonis would intentionally hurt them, but the other one would.

"That's wonderful," Mary purred. "Thank you."

"Yes, thank you," Sylvie agreed.

"You're welcome," he replied politely.

Yep, Sylvie smiled inwardly, Adonis was the weak link. They'd have him wrapped around their pinkies in no time.

"Uh, oh," Mary whimpered, looking from Adonis to Sylvie and then back again. "I have to pee."

"Mary," Sylvie hissed.

"What? I'm eighty-one years-old, and so is my bladder."

If Sylvie could have smacked her friend up side the head she would have.

"Fine, I'll take you out to pee, but don't try anything stupid," Adonis mumbled.

"How can I?" Mary scolded him as if he was a child. "I haven't run anywhere except to the bathroom in over twenty years and I really need to do that now."

"Okay, okay, don't get your panties in a twist," he mumbled, tossing Mary's sleeping bag aside, and unfastening the rope around Mary's waist.

"You'll have to cut that duck tape off my legs and help me up," Mary screeched. "I don't think I can stand. Hurry, I can't hold it much longer."

"All right," Adonis yelped, working as quickly as he could to get Mary to her feet before half carrying her out of the building.

Sylvie sat alone in the breezy room, watching a spider re-build its nest over her head. She hated spiders. As she listened to the wind in the rafters and the rain pounding against the roof, the urge to pee suddenly overwhelmed her too.

"Hey," she hollered. "I have to go too. Get back in here!"

***

Sam stood inside the barn doors, illuminated by the lights at his back, the two Saint Bernards lying at his feet. His Stetson shaded his eyes as he stared at the sparkling twilight, the stars gleaming above the thin line of pink on the western horizon. The storm had blown through in record time; either that or the system was so large they were in the eye of it. He wasn't sure. Behind him, the horses snuffled in their stalls as they settled down for the night unaware of the turmoil in the soul of the man who cared for them.

The trip into town had been a bust. The only good thing about it was that no spats had broken out. Maggie had even been civil.

The dogs stood up as the lights from an SUV rounded the bend in their drive and quietly approached the barn.

Sheriff Trane parked the Suburban and stepped out into the night, his boots clicking on the gravel beneath his feet.

"Any news," Sam asked, tossing aside the piece of straw he had been chewing on.

"State police found Mary's truck," Cole said with a glance towards the house where Emma's shadow was visible in the kitchen window.

"Where was it?"

"On the side road between the penitentiary and the high way, about a half mile from the front gate," the sheriff replied. "The hood was up and the key was in the ignition."

"Hmmmpf," Sam rumbled. "So, there was probably no doctor's appointment either?"

"Nope," Cole said with a shake of his head.

The men stood in silence for a moment. The dogs sniffed Cole and wagged their tails. He reached down and absently scratched behind the dogs ears.

"So, what do you think they were doing at the penn? I didn't have a chance to talk to the warden yet. He'd already gone home and the staff refused to call him."

"I expect the ladies went to try to talk some sense into Cortez," Sam growled. "I figure they were gonna try and get him to cancel the wedding."

"Mrs. Puddicombe wouldn't like that, I don't expect," the sheriff snorted.

"Nope, but it would be better than her cancelling on him. Women aren't known for doing the smart thing," Sam agreed, "especially not that one."

"Is she still wandering at night," Cole inquired innocently.

"Not since the doc put her on some pills to help with that," Sam admitted. "I wonder sometimes if Zoe is capable of making the right decision, but then I remind myself that I ain't her husband or her kin and it ain't my place. She's outlived three of her six husbands. It ain't a big surprise that she'd say 'I do' with a felon."

Cole nodded thoughtfully.

"Well, I'll talk to the warden tomorrow and we'll take it from there," Cole sighed. "Maybe they'll call tonight or in the morning. If they don't and let's say the worst has happened, we should have a ransom demand shortly. Still, I don't know why anyone would kidnap Mary and Sylvie."

"Me neither," Sam mumbled, tipping his hat back on his head. He had been wondering the same thing.

"I don't want to think about the other alternative," Cole sighed.

"And that is," Sam winced, knowing what Cole was about to say. He was worried about that too. What if they were taken by somebody with more than money on their mind? Mary was the oldest friend he still had left, and Sylvie... well, he was in love with Sylvie. If they were killed by some psycho serial killer, Sam wouldn't stop until he tracked him down.

"Well, let's not go there," Cole mumbled.

Sam remained silent. There was nothing more to say. He nodded goodnight to Cole and waited for the sheriff to get back into his vehicle before turning off the barn lights.

Deep in thought, Sam walked with the dogs back to the house.

He passed Emma on the way to his room. Her face was streaked with tears. He had no consolation to offer her.

The two dogs whined and galloped up the stairs, running to Mary's room, and then back to the top of the stairs where they stared down upon Sam, their eyes as droopy as their dripping jowls.

"They know something's wrong," Emma sobbed behind him.

"They do," Sam agreed.

Emma threw herself into his arms. Sam hugged her back fiercely.

"We'll find them," he croaked.

Emma nodded.

"Come on, girls, you can sleep with me tonight," Emma told the dogs as she broke away from Sam, her shoulders slumped with worry.

"Still no word?" Maggie asked from the top of the stairs, startling both Sam and Emma.

Maggie's eyes were red and swollen. It was obvious she had been crying copiously.

"No," Emma croaked, climbing the stairs. The dogs licked her hands, as worried as the rest of them.

"Cole is going to talk to the warden at the prison first thing in the morning," Sam sighed, realizing he needed to tell Maggie and Emma something. Maggie was Sylvie's best friend. The Ice Queen had a heart after all.

"Why?" Emma asked, turning to face him.

"They found Mary's truck on the ring road outside the prison," he confessed.

"They went to see Tommy," Maggie whispered, her shoulders slumping.

"Went to see Tommy about what?" Zoe queried, tying her housecoat around her slim waist as she emerged from her bedroom.

Lord, it appeared everyone was up, Sam grumbled to himself. He hoped the kids weren't.

"It appears so," Sam agreed.

"Mary and Sylvie went to see Tommy," Maggie explained to Zoe. "The sheriff found Mary's truck."

"And no sign of the ladies," Emma continued.

Sam shook his head, his sadness and anger threatening to overwhelm him.

"I know what happened," Maggie murmured. "They went to try and talk some sense into Tommy."

"Why would they do that," Zoe said, her brow knitting together in confusion.

"Because neither one of us should be marrying or coming to fist-a-cuffs over a drug smuggler who will never ever get out of prison," Maggie spat. "It's our fault, Zoe. It's our fault they went to the prison and that they have probably been abducted by some ruthless felon wanting to get back at Tommy."

"I don't understand," Zoe cried, her hand shooting out to steady herself against the wall.

Emma wrapped her arms around the distraught woman.

"Shhh, let's not wake the kids," Emma hushed Zoe.

"What I mean is whoever kidnapped Sylvie and Mary must think they are us," Maggie whispered fiercely, the fire returning to her eyes.

Sam hadn't thought of that. Maggie had a point. The ladies may have well been taken as pay-back against Tommy Cortez.

"I'm gonna go call Cole," Sam rumbled. "It's time to wake the warden. You gals head back to bed. There's nothing we can do about it right now."

Maggie and Sam's eyes met. Sam saw the cold determination in her eyes. She must have been quite the force to reckon with when she was young. Even now, the cold calculated look she gave him made him shiver.

"Come on, Zoe," Emma mumbled, "let's get you to bed. The dogs are used to sleeping with Mary. If you want, they can sleep with you?"

"No thank you," Zoe whimpered. "Maggie's right. I've a lot to think about."

"We both do," Maggie sighed heavily, placing a comforting hand on Zoe's shoulder. "The dogs can sleep with me if they want. I rather fancy the company right now."

"Okay," Emma replied, shocked. "Dozer, Junior, in with Maggie."

Maggie returned to her bedroom, the dogs exuberantly running ahead of her.

"Well, that's a first," Sam muttered, heading for the phone in the kitchen.

Sam shambled to his bedroom after calling Cole with the suggestion that he wake the warden to have a midnight chat with one of his most famous inmates, refusing to even glance sideways at the dark entryway to Sylvie's bedroom which was beside his. He sat down heavily on his bed and poured himself a stiff shot of Johnny Walker.

"Hells-bells," he grumbled, tossing back the whiskey. "I'll find you, Sylvie, I swear it on my wife's grave, and you too, Mary. God, give me strength, and while you're at it, look after those two crazy old broads for me. They're something special."

***

Benny wiped down the steering wheel and the seats of the GMC van they had stolen from A-1 Industrial Supplies with bleach. He wasn't a dummy. He had watched every episode of CSI and NCIS. Benny had even tied a plastic grocery store bag over his head so he wouldn't leave any 'trace evidence' as they called it on the show and wore thick black rubber gloves.

His father would be pleased. All he had to do now was signal him from the road outside the yard in the morning: two long flashes of his headlights and a right turn signal. That was what they had decided upon. Benny wouldn't

126

even have to enter the prison's parking lot. After that, his father would find a way to deliver the ransom note to his bunk mate, Tommy Cortez.

Yeah, baby, it was smooth sailing from here, Benny thought to himself. *What could possibly go wrong?*

Chapter Fourteen

A horse is worth more than riches.
Spanish Proverb

Tommy sat in a chair behind closed doors in front of the warden, his wrists chained to his waist.

"This is no time for you to hold back," the warden told him. "Is there anyone you can think of who might hate you enough to kidnap your fiancée and her friend? The kidnappers don't know they have the wrong women according to the sheriff, and Sheriff Trane and I both believe we need to keep that fact a secret. There are only a handful of people privy to this information."

Fury welled up inside Tommy's chest. It ate at him like a dragon clawing its way to the surface, intent on devouring everything in its path.

"Nobody I can think of," Tommy growled. "I've been out of the game a long time. I'd tell you if I knew."

Tommy didn't add that he had eliminated the most dangerous threats a year ago. He wasn't proud of the blood on his hands, but his family meant everything to him.

"You're sure?" the warden asked through gritted teeth.

"Positive, el patrón," Tommy replied.

"If a ransom demand comes in, I'll let you know and I expect the same of you," the warden wheezed. He tugged a blue inhaler out of his desk drawer and inhaled a shot of Salbutamol. "I'm not happy about this, Tommy. I can't have things like this happening on my watch. I don't want to transfer you. You've been a model prisoner, but I will if needed."

"I'm not happy about it either, Warden," Tommy grimaced, the firestorm inside not relenting. It took every ounce of his self-control to keep a handle on it.

"If anything happens in the yard, you come see me. Tell the guard it's about your wedding arrangements. I won't call the Feds until we have a ransom demand. If we call them, it'll be all over the news within the hour and we don't want the ladies put in any further danger," the warden commanded.

"Si," Tommy agreed, standing up as the warden pressed the intercom on his desk.

The warden was a slim effeminate man in his late forties with severe asthma, but he was hard and efficient when it came to running the prison. Despite his mannerisms, the inmates respected him and the guards trusted him.

The guard that responded to the call was a former Marine. The warden hadn't taken any chances relaying the news about the attempted kidnapping of Zoe and Maggie to Tommy.

"Take him back to his cell," the warden ordered the guard.

"Wedding plans, huh?" the guard whispered to Tommy as they left the warden's office.

"Yep," Tommy mumbled.

"At seven o'clock in the morning," the guard snorted in disbelief.

"Warden's a busy man, gotta catch him when you can," Tommy said, shuffling down the hall to the elevator. The warden's office overlooked the yard. It was a long way from his cell block.

Tommy noticed the end of a white envelope peeking out from beneath the corner of his pillow when the guard let him back into his cell. The cell door was open as were the others on the block, the inmates having gone to the cafeteria for breakfast. His cellmate was also gone. Anyone could have left the note there, a guard or an inmate. Perhaps the warden had been right in keeping the guards uninformed? The warden was no dummy. Anyone, prisoner or guard, could be behind this.

"Thanks," Tommy nodded to the guard as he unfastened the cuffs around Tommy's wrists.

"Good luck with the planning," the guard commented dryly.

Tommy waited until the guard was long gone before grabbing the envelope. He flipped it over and examined it. There was nothing on the outside or the underside – no name, no marks, just a regular No. 10 white business envelope. It wasn't even sealed.

Smart, Tommy mused, no DNA.

Tommy pulled the folded nine and a half by eleven inch piece of alabaster paper from inside the envelope and read the note inside. It was short and to the point.

"Three million in three days or the broads die. I'll be in touch."

Plain. Simple. Printed out on a computer, not hand written. Interesting choice of words – not 'ladies die' or 'girlfriends die', not even 'your fiancée dies' – and no way to contact the jerk.

Tommy tore the envelope and ransom note into shreds and flushed it down the toilet.

It was an inmate who wrote the note, Tommy was certain of it.

At least Zoe and Maggie were safe. That was a blessing. Neither would forgive him though if he didn't come up with the ransom money for their friends' sake.

He had the money. That wasn't an issue. The issue was that it was hidden with the only friend he had left in Mexico. JJ would be arrested and probably executed if he went to Mexico to retrieve it; neither the police nor the cartel would allow it. Marco wouldn't trust Sam Montana; Montana was too John Wayne. The alternative made him blanch. She was tough though. If anyone had the guts to cross the border secretly to retrieve the money, it was Maggie.

"Mierda," he swore.

"Something wrong," his cellmate asked, wandering into the cell from the showers. Park always showered before breakfast and for some unknown reason, the guards let him. He probably used Tommy's name. Right now, the thought and the smell of Ivory soap drifting off the fat man was irritating.

"Why are you asking, cabrón?" Tommy snarled.

"Whoa, whoa. You just look a little pale, is all."

"These wedding plans are driving me loco," Tommy lied.

Park laughed and slapped Tommy on the back.

Tommy didn't like Park, but as a cellmate he was okay, except for throwing Tommy's name around far too casually. The warden was right. Tommy had to be careful, and suspicious of everyone, especially Bruce Park, inmate number 84958. He'd call JJ after breakfast, tell him what was going on, and ask him to go talk to Maggie privately.

"Guess I should go eat something, keep my strength up for my wedding night," Tommy said, grinning like a wolf in the middle of lambing season.

Park laughed aloud and the two men sauntered down the hall to the cafeteria like they were the top of the food chain. In Tommy's case, he was. Parks was as big a joke inside the prison as the scrambled eggs.

***

Nausea rumbled through JJ's stomach as he hung up his cell phone. What was his father thinking? Seriously, he thought an old lady capable of meeting up with Uncle Marco, a coyote JJ barely remembered, to sneak three million dollars in ransom money across the border without getting caught?

"Madre de Dios, what am I going to do," the young man muttered, rubbing a hand through his short cropped hair as he stared at the phone number he had scribbled on the hotel's stationary pad on the desk.

Despite his father's words, he would have to tell someone about his father's crazy plan, but whom? Not Emma, she would dismiss it outright. The sheriff? No way. He could tell Sam, but Sam would probably throw him off the property.

There were no other options but to follow his father's instructions. He'd have to call Uncle Marco first and make the arrangements. JJ's stomach soured. There would be no more horseback rides with the beautiful Emma after this.

Damn the Cortez name, he should have changed it to his mother's maiden name like his older brother did.

***

"We need to call Gus and Dee," Emma whispered dejectedly to Sam over a cup of coffee. "I'm sure they'll help and I trust them."

She had whisked the kids off to school, assuring them Sylvie and Mary had gone to Las Vegas for a couple of days to see a show and not to worry. Jenny had cried about not getting a hug from her two cowgirl grandmas before leaving, but an extra few pieces of bacon on toast had solved that problem. Maggie and Zoe hadn't come down for breakfast yet. Those two were the larger issue.

"Dee can keep an eye out on her rounds for anything suspicious and maybe Gus can track them down," Emma explained. "I mean, it is his specialty, tracking fugitives."

"Dee, I can see, but I'm not sure about Gus," Sam agreed. "He may have to report it to his superiors and we need to keep the abduction out of the news. Cole and his men know what is at stake. The deputies are trackers too."

"Gus will keep quiet if we ask him to," Emma said.

There was a soft knock on the front door.

"Come in," Sam shouted without getting up.

JJ slunk into the kitchen, his face ashen.

"Sorry to barge in without phoning first, but I need to talk to you both," JJ groaned. "My father has placed me in an impossible position and I don't know what to do. I was going to follow his wishes, but it didn't seem right."

"Sit down before you fall down, son," Sam offered, pulling out a chair.

A big fat lump rose into Emma's throat. There was no hint of humour in JJ's dark brown eyes this morning, no slight curl of a smile on his lips. His face was pale, and eyes downcast. She shivered uncontrollably.

"Has something happened to your dad?" she stuttered.

"No, but he received a ransom demand early this morning," JJ moaned.

"So, Mary and Sylvie were kidnapped," Sam grumbled, closing his eyes, his whole body quaking.

"They were," JJ confirmed. "My dad found a ransom note under his pillow asking for three million dollars in three days after he met with the warden. The warden informed him about keeping it quiet because the kidnappers didn't know they took the wrong women."

"And the warden is keeping quiet too, I hope," Maggie retorted, barrelling into the room, the two Saint Bernards frolicking beside her. The dogs wagged their tails, approaching everyone at the table, looking for love and attention.

"He is," JJ nodded. "The warden doesn't know about the ransom note and my father doesn't want him to. Someone at the prison is involved. My father is pretty sure its an inmate."

"Well, we don't have three million dollars," Emma declared, fear making her fidget in her seat. She pushed Bulldozer's head out of her lap.

"I don't either," Maggie grumbled, taking a seat at the table. "I have enough to look after myself in the manner I am used to, but none to spare."

"I'm afraid I don't either," Zoe quipped, striding into the kitchen with purpose.

Emma noticed Zoe had covered her black eye with makeup. Her freshly moussed her hair looked like porcupine quills. She was dressed to kill in a smart bolero jacket and sparkly studded jeans.

Maggie simply raised an eyebrow. She still wore her black silk nightgown.

"We do," JJ sighed. "That is where the problem lies."

"Here it comes," Sam said gruffly.

Emma folded one hand over his. The shattered look in her father in-law's eyes spoke volumes.

"Papa's stash is in Mexico. Uncle Marco knows where it is. He used to work for my dad. The problem is that I can't cross the border. My father has an agreement with the cartel that neither he nor any of his family would ever go there again and they'd leave us alone. That was why he was flying up to stay with my sister last summer when his plane crashed."

"I see," Sam sputtered, his eyes narrowing. "You want me to go get it."

"No, not you," JJ mumbled.

Emma wanted to race to JJ's side and cuddle his head against her chest like she did with her kids when they were sick. Probably not a good idea, she reasoned.

Why was it that the Universe kept sending her these tall dark and handsome men? First it was Gus, but she had turned him away in favour of Cole when jealousy got the better of her. In reality, it was Cole who should be here, sitting in on this meeting and comforting them all.

A hurricane of guilt threatened to overwhelm her. She should be thinking of Sylvie and Mary, not which man she wanted to date or continue dating. What was wrong with her?

"It's me," Maggie chortled, her brown eyes alive with mirth and intelligence. "I'm the one Tommy wants to send to Mexico."

"Don't be ridiculous, it's me he wants to go," Zoe purred.

"Now who's being silly, you're not strong enough," Maggie replied, dismissing the notion with a wave of her hand. "Tommy knows I can be ruthless if need be."

"Either way, that's not happening," Sam snorted. "Neither of you are jumping the border to bring back three million dollars in drug money."

"That is not your decision to make, Sam Montana," Maggie replied confidently. "My best friend's life is at stake. I'll go. All I need is directions and a contact number."

"I don't care what you say, I'm going with you," Zoe announced, tapping her foot annoyingly. "You can't stop me."

Sam rubbed his forehead. The veins in his temple were throbbing.

JJ sunk deep into his chair.

Emma didn't know what to say. Part of her was relieved that Tommy was ready to fork over the money for Sylvie and Zoe's release, and that Maggie and Zoe were prepared to go to Mexico to retrieve it, but the rest of her was numb. My god, these women were so brave, but then if one of her children had been kidnapped, or her friend, Dee Gallant, Emma knew she would do anything to get them back.

"If you're sure, I'll call Uncle Marco, and tell him you're coming," JJ said to Maggie and Zoe, standing up. "There's a spot we can sneak you across the border. I'll drop you off. It is a long drive though so we will have to leave right away to make the kidnapper's deadline. Uncle Marco or one of his sons will meet us at the crossing."

"Wild horses aren't going to stop me, Sam, and neither are you so put that thought to bed," Maggie commanded, seemingly happy.

Maggie seemed thrilled at the adventure, Emma realized. Maggie was a force of nature. Emma pitied the man who got in her way. Maggie was capable of murder, she had tried it before.

Emma let out a shaky breath. Maggie was a lot like Tommy, and Tommy knew that. That was why Tommy wanted Maggie to go. Zoe was another matter. Zoe was the fly in the ointment.

A chill as frigid as a frosty morning swept over her. Maybe she should broach the subject with Sam: should they let Maggie and Sylvie continue to reside under their roof? They had Jenny and BJ to consider. No matter how much she admired Maggie's determination or pitied Sylvie's heartbreak, they were scary at times.

Chapter Fifteen

The merry-go-round was running…yes, but.. it was running backwards.
Ray Bradbury. *Running, moon, cymbals.*

Dee galloped up the steep mountain slope, the shale crumbling beneath her horse's hooves. The bay gelding she rode was a sturdy mustang. A brand ran along the upper part of his arched neck. He snorted and lifted his tail. His ears were pricked forward as they climbed higher and higher to a vantage point she knew would give them a clear view of the valley and part of the upper slopes of the mountain ranges that stretched in either direction.

Gus was flying in later that evening. He had dropped everything when Dee called him and told him about the missing women. He had taken two weeks leave, promising he wouldn't tell his superiors why he needed to go on such short notice. Dee prayed it wouldn't take that long to find the ladies.

The pretty ranger reined up atop the flat knoll she had ridden her horse hard to arrive at. The views from the plateau didn't disappoint.

Dee had a hunch the kidnappers were holding the ladies in the mountains. The town wasn't very big so it made sense to head to the hills. Of course, she realized, the women could be hidden someplace closer to the prison given that was where their truck was found, but it seemed unlikely given how busy the area was.

The mountain range was the likely hidey-hole.

"Easy, Bingo," she whispered to the mustang, stroking his neck. She had chosen this stocky boy over her Quarter horse because of his tough compact body build. Her Quarter horse was what they called a running Quarter horse, fast and with amazing staying power, but the mustang was as sure footed as a mountain goat. She had bought him at auction last fall. He was tough to train, and had tested her patience, but the bond the two now shared was worth more than gold.

Dee felt the horse sigh with pleasure as he stood on the knoll, his neck and hind quarters flecked with sweat. He gave out a loud snort and shook himself, almost sending Dee careening out of the saddle.

The ranger laughed and stroked his neck before pulling a set of high powered binoculars out of her saddle bag.

Dee lifted the binoculars and looked around. Herds of deer grazed along the Diamond Bar and Montana ranches borders. There were at least a dozen different herds of four to seven animals. The entrance to the old mine was also visible, the black hole that led into the main shaft looking like the end of a rifle barrel at that distance.

From this vantage point, she could also see the church steeple in town. She let her gaze travel over the highway and up the road she had marked out for the upcoming donkey race. She still couldn't believe she had agreed to manage it.

Dee zeroed in on the structures in the ramshackle mining town. There was nothing out of place – no trucks or ATVs anywhere near it. The rain last night had washed away any tracks so if someone was driving in and out, she wouldn't see any evidence of activity. The decrepit town was too popular anyway. It would be a stupid place to hide someone.

She put down the binoculars.

Farther up the mountain was a second ranger cabin. One could only get to it by horse or by foot so it seemed an unlikely place, but she would have preferred to check it out. It was another half hour ride. If she didn't head back now, she would be late for her park ranger's meeting and Gus' plane's arrival.

"Come on, Bingo," she murmured, "it's time to head home."

The mustang shook his head as if saying 'no'. Dee smiled. Another time and another place, she would have let the mustang have his way, but not today.

***

Percy was furious.

Where was Benny?

Benny was supposed to bring them breakfast, but never showed up. Thankfully, Percy had stocked a bunch of energy bars, juice and water in the abandoned hotel.

It had been a long night. Every time, he got settled down and closed his eyes, one of the ladies had to pee. It was unnerving how much water those two dames passed.

"I don't suppose we could fire up this here woodstove and boil some water, eh?" Sylvie asked.

"Oh, I'd kill for a cup of coffee," Mary agreed.

"Coffee's bad for you," Percy replied absently.

"You know, I think you should let us go," Sylvie entreated. "Your buddy has obviously abandoned you."

"Or one of Tommy's friends got to him," Mary agreed. "Bet he's buzzard bait."

"You know I think you're right, Zoe," Sylvie grinned, keeping in character. "Didn't Tommy say that the boys were all coming in for the wedding? I bet they're already here."

"He did say that, didn't he," Mary nodded vigorously.

"Stop it," Percy seethed.

Percy paced the floor.

The broads had a point. What if Cortez's family and men were in town for the upcoming nuptials? Maybe Benny was tied up somewhere getting tortured? What would happen to him if they found him with the ladies?

Percy paled.

There was no way he was going to go up against a line of seasoned killers. Man, all he wanted was enough money to open his gym. Damn, Benny. He should have walked away from this gig.

"I still think Adonis here is a nice kid," Sylvie informed her friend.

"I agree, Mags," Mary replied. "I hope the boys make it quick."

"Enough already," Percy spat, bolting out of the room.

Percy flung open the back door to the hotel. The afternoon was clouding over. It was going to be another wet and windy day. If Benny didn't bring something hot to eat soon, maybe he'd walk out to the highway and hitch a ride. He could phone the cops after he'd skipped town and tell them where to find the old ladies. He wasn't as heartless as Benny. He'd make sure someone found them.

A wolf jogged out of the brush beside the road. It stopped and sniffed the air, the hair on its back rising. The wolf turned and saw Percy. Yellow eyes stared right into his soul.

Okay, he thought, maybe he'd wait a little longer for Benny to arrive. If he didn't show by tomorrow morning, he'd cut loose and run.

"Oh, sweetie, I have to do a number two," the lady Benny thought was Zoe yelled at him.

There was no way he was going to wipe an old lady' bottom, Percy fumed. Nope, not doing it, he simmered.

Chapter Sixteen

*Leave a horse's gate unfastened and he'll be knocking on your
window in the night.*

JJ drove Maggie and Zoe to the border where the tunnel
between Mexico and the USA that his father had been
using for years was located. JJ had thought it had been
dynamited closed, but his uncle had assured him it was
still open.

JJ had returned the economy car he had rented for a four
wheel drive. The road they were on now was more of a
goat trail than a road. He followed the GPS coordinates his
uncle had given him, praying that the GPS wouldn't take
him off course as had been known to happen.

The ladies had been silent the whole eight hour drive,
whether that was due to fear or because they simply
couldn't stand each other was anyone's guess. They could
have flown, but his father told him it was safer to drive.

He had to dodge border patrols a couple of times during the night, but the fact they hadn't seen other headlights for the past hour was a plus.

JJ glanced at the clock: it was four in the morning. It was a good time for a border crossing.

"You are at your destination," the GPS voice announced.

"Well, ladies, this is it," he said, parking the SUV beside a giant yucca. "Are you sure you want to do this? I don't mind turning around."

"No, we're not backing out now, our friends' lives are in our hands," Maggie sighed wearily from the passenger seat beside him.

"The one thing I haven't figured out yet is why your uncle couldn't bring the money to the border and we'd pick it up here," Zoe noted, leaning forward in the back seat.

"He told me he was being watch," JJ replied. "I asked the same question."

"If he's being watched, then how will we retrieve the money," Maggie demanded, turning in her seat to face him.

"I asked that too," JJ continued. "He told me his son will take you to pick up the cash and then bring you back here. I will be back here in twenty-four hours to pick you up."

Maggie harrumphed and pushed open the passenger door. Zoe did the same in the back seat.

JJ stepped out of the Jeep and walked around to the back hatch. He opened it and pulled out three extra large canvas shoulder bags.

"Now, the money that you're bringing back will be in large dominations so the three bags should be more than enough. Uncle Marco has already seen to that. It shouldn't matter because you're going to have an escort all the way there and back."

"That's what I'm worried about," Maggie grumbled.

"You're sure these men are trustworthy?" Zoe worried.

"I swear on my life you will be safe," JJ assured the two women.

Would they though, JJ asked himself, *would they be safe?* He hadn't seen his Uncle Marco in twenty years and had never met his sons. JJ meant what he said: he would cross the border to find them, despite the threats to his personal safety. The two old women standing in front of him staring into the darkness without so much as a shiver of fear deserved his loyalty.

A thin beam of light flashed three times to the south of their position.

"That's him," JJ whispered, stepping away from the Jeep.

Maggie and Zoe followed wordlessly behind him, their heads held high.

"JJ," his Uncle Marco greeted him.

"Uncle? It's you!"

"Si, we did the old bait and switch so I could meet you without being followed," Marco laughed lightly. "I did not want these fine ladies to think bad of us, eh?"

Tommy grinned, relief flooding through him.

"Miss Maggie, Miss Zoe, meet my Uncle Marco," JJ introduced the ladies.

"Senioritas," Marco replied, bowing to first Maggie and then Zoe.

"Muy bueno, they are very beautiful," Marco whispered to JJ.

"They are," JJ agreed.

"If you have cell phones on you, you must give them to JJ," Marco demanded. "The police and border agents, they can track cell phones."

The alarm bells went off in JJ's head.

"I am not giving up my phone," Maggie seethed.

"If you want to live, you will," Marco replied, his palms open in supplication.

"I hate it, but it makes sense," JJ nodded.

Maggie begrudgingly pulled her phone out of the small purse she carried.

"And yours," Marco said, looking pointedly at Zoe.

"Oh, I don't have one anymore," the spiky haired woman shrugged.

"Come, we must hurry," Marco said, waving the ladies to the tunnel beneath the eighteen foot wall. "It will be light soon."

"Okay," JJ stammered. "Ready ladies?"

Maggie waived him away and stepped down into the black hole beneath the ground, two empty shoulder bags bounced lightly against her back as she walked, the thin beam of Marco's flashlight in front of her the only thing lighting the way.

Zoe paused. She looked from JJ to the tunnel, sighed in defeat and followed after Maggie's retreating back.

"Mother Mary protect them," JJ mumbled, crossing himself.

***

Tommy lay in bed, hands behind his head, staring at the underside of the top bunk. His cellmate snored lightly in his sleep. The click of a guard's boots on linoleum echoed down the cell block as the guard completed his rounds.

Tommy was wide awake despite the late hour. He thought of his beautiful fiancée and equally beautiful girlfriend striding through the underground tunnel beneath the wall, bravely entering the coyote's den.

He hated himself for asking them to do this, but whoever was behind the kidnapping had to be close to him. They knew he would pay anything to get his women back. Tommy might be marrying Zoe, but he loved the raven haired temptress just as much.

Tommy had a few suspects in mind: the cartel because they wanted to change their agreement, his very own cellmate, or the pony tailed lifer who dared to sit beside him like he was a long lost buddy. There may even be someone else he hadn't noticed sticking their noses in his business.

As he listened to the guard's footsteps disappear into the distance and the metal door at the end of the block slide open and closed, he smiled crookedly.

Tommy slipped out of his bunk, grabbed a pillow and stood up. He placed the pillow over his cellmate's face and held on tight.

Bruce Park gagged, his hands flailing about wildly as he gripped Tommy's arms and tried to get free.

Just when Park was about to go limp, Tommy released the pillow. Park inhaled sharply. Tommy leaned forward until he was inches from his face.

"I know you did it," Tommy growled. "The question is, do you feel lucky? You got what, five years left? That's a lot of time to get even."

"What the heck," Park stammered, gulping for air. "I don't know what you're talking about. I haven't done anything. Okay, maybe I pinched a bar of your soap last week, but that's all, I swear it. I'll get you a new one."

"That's good, Brucie," Tommy whispered, "because I got time on my hands, lots and lots of time."

Tommy released the pressure around his bunkmate's neck.

"I want you to listen up when you're in the yard or in the grub line, you hear me?"

Park nodded his eyes wide with fear. Sweat beaded his forehead.

"Anyone talks about me, no matter how small the comment, I want to know about it, got it," Tommy threatened. "I want you to find out more about this guy, a lifer with a pony tail, big guy, with an alcoholic's nose."

"Oh, yeah," Bruce replied, his head bouncing up and down like a yoyo. "I know the guy you mean. He killed some guy on a race course. I think it was a jockey. They were running some kind of scam and the jockey wanted out. I don't remember his name."

149

"That's good, amigo," Tommy said, nodding encouragement.

The horse connection was interesting. Maybe the kidnapping was related to one of the ladies and not just him as everyone assumed. That hadn't occurred to him. Maybe he would toss that tidbit to the warden, get him off his back.

***

Bruce Park sweated as he tried to calm his nerves. He had thought Tommy had figured it out, but Cortez was just fishing.

Once his heart stopped racing, he smirked.

When the ransom was paid and he had a chance to talk to his son, he was going to tell Benny to off the old broads and the creepy steroid buddy he was chumming around with. He didn't want any loose ends. It'd serve Tommy right too, thinking he could lay his hands on him like that.

There was no way Tommy would ever find out the brains behind the kidnapping was none other than Bruce Park, his best buddy.

Hah, maybe the cartel would pay him a bonus for taking Cortez down, then who would be the big man for the next five years!

Chapter Seventeen

Been there…jumped that!

The morning sun shone through the papered windows in the front room. It was still chilly inside the building, but it was gradually warming up. The ladies were curled up like kittens on the floor inside their sleeping bags. He had stopped bothering to tape up their legs. They weren't going anywhere, and neither was he.

Percy heard the rumble of an engine and the squeal of tires on gravel outside.

"About time," he grumbled, shuffling to the back door. Looking after the two super seniors was as tiring as training for a weight lifting competition, made all the more miserable by the fact none of them had had a hot meal or a cup of coffee or tea in almost two days.

He was about to shout out his annoyance when he stopped short. It wasn't Benny's beat up Bronco outside the building; it was a giant work truck pulling a trailer with two porta-potties tied to it. Percy jumped back into the shadows of the doorway, careful to remain unseen.

He watched as two men unloaded the porta-potties into the log corral, setting them down on a couple of wood pallets and then filling up the johns with rolls of toilet paper and bottles of hand sanitizer.

What are they doing that for, he wondered. *They were in an abandoned town in the middle of nowhere. Why was there a need for toilets all of a sudden?*

Satisfied the porta-potties were level, the men jumped back into the truck and were off, heading back they way they came.

Percy strolled out of the hotel, shading his eyes from the sun, and wandered over to the porta-potties. The little green huts appeared brand spanking new. He smiled as he opened the door; at least he wouldn't have to hold the ladies up as they relieved themselves in the bushes anymore, plus they now had toilet paper.

As he sat on the john, Percy realized one thing: he could have asked for a lift into town and been done with this whole fiasco.

***

Emma saw her reflection in the window. Her eyes were rimmed with dark circles and her curly mane of red hair looked like she had just got out of bed. She hadn't; she'd been up for hours.

She was just about to go back to sleep after Cole left when JJ phoned to tell her not to worry, his uncle had picked Zoe and Maggie up himself. She felt a little better, but the nightmare she had a few hours earlier haunted her like a song that got stuck in one's head and just wouldn't go away.

The house seemed empty with only the family in it.

Once again, she and Sam had lied to the kids. It broke Sam and her hearts to do so, but it was for the best. They told the kids Maggie and Zoe had decided to join Mary and Sylvie in Vegas for a couple of days.

Jenny bounced into the kitchen.

"Are you ready for school?" Emma asked.

"Mom, its Saturday," Jenny scolded her mother.

"That's right, I forgot," Emma winced.

"Do you think we can make candy apples today," Jenny asked, pouring herself a glass of orange juice.

"Sure," Emma quickly agreed. "How many do you want?"

"Maybe four," the little girl said, wrinkling her nose, deep in thought.

"And who are these candy apples for," Emma chuckled, her daughter's enthusiasm making the world a little brighter.

"Mike," Jenny grinned.

"Oh, no, I am not making candy apples for a donkey," Emma said. "They'll rot his teeth and he already has a hard time eating."

"I wasn't planning on feeding them to him," her daughter wheedled. "I was going to put them on a stick in front of his face like I saw in a cartoon once. If he doesn't learn to run faster we won't win the race."

"No," Emma said, hands on her hips. "You are not going to dangle a candy apple in front of Mike's face to make him run faster. He will run as fast as he wants to and that is all there is to it!"

"But, Moooommmm," Jenny wailed.

"Don't 'but' your mother," Sam warned his granddaughter as he walked into the room buttoning up his shirt. "It's the weekend and you got chores. I suggest you get out to the barn and help your brother. No belly aching about it either."

"You guys are so mean," Jenny grumbled as her grandfather swatted her lightly on the behind to get her moving.

"Any news from Cole or Dee," Emma asked her father in-law. She had tried to get another hour sleep at Sam's urging. Maybe she had fallen asleep for awhile and her friends had called.

"Dee picked up Gus at the airport last night. His plane was late," he nodded, pouring himself a cup of coffee. "She said they didn't get home until a couple of hours ago. They are going to get some shut eye and will be by to pick up BJ and Bucky around noon."

"Pick up BJ? Why?" Emma gasped. She didn't think the pit in her stomach could get any bigger but it did.

"They need to flag the trails for the donkey race. The race is next weekend. The committee moved it up on account of too many entries and not enough donkeys to go around."

Emma collapsed at the kitchen table, a hand over her mouth. Tears welled in her eyes.

"Don't worry, Gus is going with them. They're going to scout the area while they're flagging the trail," Sam consoled her.

"What about Cole," she squeaked.

"Cole phoned too. He got the results back on the finger prints they lifted inside the truck. There weren't any hits. The ones they found matched up to the ones he took this morning from inside Mary's and Sylvie's rooms."

"Okay. I was hoping Cole'd find something. I guess I'll make some extra sandwiches for Dee, Gus and BJ to take with them," Emma sobbed, brushing the tears from her face.

"Make them for four," Sam suggested. "I'm going with them."

"Okay," she nodded. "I think I can keep Jenny occupied for the afternoon. We'll look after the horses."

Sam grinned and kissed her on top of the head.

Just as he did that, a loud gunshot echoed through the house. Emma bolted out of her chair. She and Sam raced to the door.

Jenny stood in the yard, a smoking cap pistol in one hand, head tucked down between her shoulders, a sorrowful look on her face. Mike stood beside her, head straight up, nostrils flared, eyes rolling in their sockets, his one ear waving in the air like a willow tree in a hurricane. The lead line fixed to his rope halter was stretched taut. It hung in the air between the donkey and the child like a newly installed clothesline.

The two dogs disappeared behind the barn, tails between their legs. The stallions galloped full tilt around their pastures. The pregnant filly trotted circles in her paddock. The ranch horses continued to graze calmly in the field.

"Is everyone okay," BJ yelled, rushing out of the barn, a pitch fork in his hand.

"I'm sorry, I thought maybe a loud noise would make Mike run since I didn't have any candy apples," Jenny whimpered.

"You are so grounded, young lady," Emma hissed.

"And where did you get that cap pistol," Sam fumed, striding towards Jenny.

"In the barn," she sobbed. "I didn't think it would be that loud."

"Well, it was," Emma smirked. "I almost had a heart attack."

"I'm sorry, I won't do it again," Jenny pleaded, her voice warbling.

"Darn right you won't," Sam growled taking the pistol from her. "Didn't I tell you to help your brother with the chores?"

"Yes'um," Jenny sniffed.

"Sorry, Mike," she told her donkey. The donkey's ear stopped windmilling and he let out a sad heart breaking bray.

"Come on, I'll walk you to the barn," Sam offered. "I know you really want to win, but let's not lose sight of the fact Mike's an old man. I don't reckon I could run five miles either."

"Not even with a candy apple on a rope in front of your nose?" Jenny asked hopefully.

"Not even then," Sam laughed.

BJ waved to his mother, and then turned on his heel and returned to the barn. There were still stalls to clean.

Emma let out a long winded sigh and went back into the house. She had lunch to make for the boys and a whopper of a headache pounding against the inside of her skull.

As she busied herself in the kitchen, she remembered her nightmares, the early morning visit, and some of the worries she had put to rest.

Emma woke from the nightmare in a sweat. She had dreamed that Zoe and Maggie were lying dead in the desert. That scene had morphed into a shadowy room where Sylvie and Mary were bound together on two chairs beneath a solitary light hanging from the ceiling. The two women were unconscious, their faces deathly pale, their lips cracked, and their bodies clinging to life.

It took her a moment to distinguish the rectangle of light blazing beneath her bedroom door from the single light bulb hanging from the ceiling in her dream, to the soft whisper of masculine voices in the hallway outside her door.

She rolled over and glanced at her alarm clock. It was five in the morning.

Emma stepped out of bed and donned the pink fuzzy nightgown and slippers she loved so much. The kids had given them to her for Christmas. A tiny white unicorn and rainbow was stitched on each pocket.

She opened the door and saw Cole bent over the dresser in Zoe's room. He was gathering hair samples from a hair brush and bagging them. Sam watched from the hallway.

"What's going on?" she whispered, tugging her dressing gown tightly around her waist. Ice ran through her veins as she watched Cole work.

"Cole needs finger prints and DNA," Sam muttered.

"Oh, no, you didn't find their...," 'bodies', Emma didn't say.

"No, honey," Cole croaked, tucking the plastic baggie in his pocket. He strode into the hall. "I just need to match up the evidence we found in Mary's truck. That way we can eliminate Mary's and Sylvie's fingerprints and focus on what the kidnappers may have left behind."

Emma shivered. Cole was so calm. Emma found herself leaning into Cole instead of her father in-law for support. The nightmare was still fresh in her mind.

Cole wrapped his arms around her.

"Listen, we have a couple of leads," he crooned in her ear. "A blue GMC cargo van was seen parked on the side road where we found Mary's truck. The same color of van was stolen from an industrial park by the airport. My guys are out looking for it now."

"We can make a couple of calls to our neighbours to ask them to keep a look out, Cole," Sam offered.

"Right now, let's keep it to just you, me and my deputies," Cole nodded, hugging Emma tight. "We'll find them."

Emma stared up into Cole's boyish face. His look softened as the love left unspoken tugged at her heart strings. She realized that she was such a fool. The Universe had already spoken. She simply had to let go and see what was right in front of her: a good man, devoted to her and the kids, both caring and thoughtful beyond all measure.

"Okay," she murmured. "You continue what you're doing and I'll go put a pot of coffee on. If you're going to work all night, I can at least make sure you have something hot to take with you."

Cole kissed her, his lips caressing her own tenderly. Emma's heart fluttered. She was still a silly girl sometime.

Sam coughed lightly.

"Sorry, Sam," Cole grinned.

"Now that's settled," Sam winked at Emma, "how about I help you with the coffee and we let Cole get back to it."

Emma snorted in amusement and turned to head down the stairs when the two dogs emerged from Maggie's bedroom. They had evidently been keeping Maggie's bed warm for her, puzzled by the change in routine. Maggie's bedroom door gaped open.

Sam looked at Emma in alarm.

"Come on you two," she chirped, rushing to shut the door behind the dogs, lest Cole notice the empty bed. "Don't wake the ladies."

Emma felt her cheeks flush. She bit her lip, praying that Cole hadn't noticed. She needn't have worried. The sheriff was already back in Mary's room with a fingerprint kit.

"That was close," Sam groaned as he put a hand on the small of Emma's back and escorted her to the stairs.

"Far too close," she responded, waving the dogs ahead of her.

The calamity of events made her grateful for her family, the ranch, the crazy group of old women she shared her home with, and Cole Trane, aka 'The Cole Trane' as they called him on the high school football team. Who knew an engagement, a kidnapping, a trail ride with a roguishly handsome mechanic, and a tortuous nightmare, could spin her life so out of control? Emma would have laughed, except it wasn't funny. No wonder she had a migraine.

Chapter Eighteen

A stubborn horse walks behind you, an impatient horse walks in front of you, but a noble companion walks beside you.

Maggie glanced over at Zoe crammed between Maggie and Marco in one of the smallest and ricketiest single cab pickup trucks on the face of the planet. Zoe's eyes were closed, her mouth slightly open, as she slept through the hair-raising drive over the rough terrain on the way to God-only-knows-where.

It was difficult to remain mute as they headed south by south-east over dusty roads and a lunar style terrain. Another time, another place, she may have enjoyed the bright red and orange hues of the magnificent sunrise over the desert, but her back ached, her lungs and nostrils were clogged with sand, and she was fighting the overwhelming urge to close her eyes and fall into a deep slumber. She didn't dare sleep. One of them needed to have some idea of the direction they were travelling in case Tommy's friend wasn't as good a friend as he was supposed to be.

Fearless didn't mean stupid. At fifteen, Maggie had shattered her left shoulder, arm and leg in a spectacular fall. She had learned a painful lesson from it. The decision to retrieve Tommy's loot was based solely on loyalty to Sylvie, not because of a self-destructive streak.

Okay, maybe it was also the need for revenge. The idea of cleaning Tommy out by delivering his stash to the kidnappers was smugly satisfying given the rock on Zoe's finger. At least, Zoe had taken it off before they left the ranch.

"Not far now," Marco said, eyeing Maggie.

Maggie got the distinct feeling the old bandit wanted a piece of her. That wasn't going to happen. He was uglier than Tommy and had none of the charisma, charm, or confidence.

Maggie knew she was still beautiful. It cost a pretty penny to uphold appearances. The Spanish and Cherokee bloodlines she inherited from her mother's side of the family were flawless. It was the Irish blood that was the problem, but hey, who didn't blame everything on the Irish?

Still, she didn't like the bandit's unwanted attention. There was nothing flattering about the way he kept glancing sideways at her.

"So, Marco, what exactly did you do for Tommy," Maggie queried. "JJ said you smuggled people over the border, but there must be more to you than a simple coyote if Tommy trusted you to hide his retirement funds."

Marco grinned like a Pit-bull Terrier.

Maggie's eyes narrowed. She could see the wheels turning as the red sunrise cast a devilish glow across Marco's face.

"I was very good at making people disappear," he replied after a moment.

"I see," Maggie nodded, forcing her expression to remain blank.

Did he intend to disappear Maggie and Zoe? It seemed unlikely, but the hair rising on the back of her neck indicated otherwise.

"You know, like giving them new identities for when they crossed the border," the bandit back-pedaled.

"Ahhh," she murmured.

Zoe snorted herself awake.

"What did I miss," her friend asked sleepily.

"A lovely sunrise," Maggie purred. "Marco says we're almost there."

"That's marvellous," Zoe purred. "Thank you, Marco, I don't know what we would have done without you."

Maggie fought the urge to smack Zoe upside the head once again. Zoe was such a ditz sometimes. She guessed men found it charming; Maggie found it irritating, especially when she had been up all night being the cautious one.

"De nada, Seniorita, we are heading to Esperanza. It is a village that is no more. It was destroyed during the Great War between our two countries. Everyone was slaughtered," Marco said, crossing himself. "It is... what do you call it... a site of great importance?"

"A heritage site," Maggie informed him.

"Si, a heritage site."

"Esperanza? That is a coincidence. Esperanza was the name of my filly's mother," Zoe cried, sitting up straighter. "It means 'hope', Maggie."

"A good omen then," Marco nodded vigorously.

Maggie wanted to wipe the smirk off the bandit's face and stuff a fist down Zoe's.

Ugh, she needed some sleep!

They continued on for another couple of hours. Maggie fought to stay conscious, but her eyelids kept drooping. Marco's idea of 'close' and her idea of 'close' were completely different.

The pickup truck squealed as Marco hung a hard right around a craggy rock face and they started to descend down a steep road towards the ruins of a small village nestled on the banks of a meandering river.

The river was both narrow and shallow, the water a dark brown brackish color. A herd of feral sheep and burros grazed the green grasses on the banks.

"Oh, aren't those burros adorable, Mags?" Zoe cried excitedly. "Don't they remind you of Mike? Jenny would love them. She'd find a way to take them home with her if she was here."

This time Maggie did roll her eyes. They weren't tourists! They had a mission to accomplish.

"They are wild and loco," Marco warned, "you must stay away from them. They will hurt you."

"They wouldn't hurt me," Zoe huffed. "All animals like me."

"We're not here to make friends with wild burros," Maggie seethed.

"You're right, I guess," Zoe sighed.

Marco was silent as he drove down into the village, stopping the truck in front of a large fountain in the middle of the square.

"Come, let's do this," the retired smuggler said as he shut off the engine and stepped out of the cab.

He offered Maggie his hand, put she ignored it, preferring instead to shove Zoe out the passenger door and scoot across the seat after her.

Maggie looked around. The sun was high overhead. It chased away the shadows in the few pueblos that were still standing. Most were in ruins. A few wood rail hitching posts fought to stay upright. The temperature was rising dramatically as the day progressed.

She had to admit it was a pretty little place.

Cactus flowers bloomed. Frogs croaked. A light breeze kissed the tops of the willows and sage that grew along the river and amongst the ruins.

The water in the terracotta fountain was murky. A myriad of bugs and tadpoles skittered above and below the surface.

She heard the scrape of metal and turned to see Marco pulling a shovel out of the back of the truck. The blade was rusted, but the edge was freshly sharpened, the silver metal gleaming.

"We have to dig it up," Marco smiled warmly. Maggie didn't believe him.

The short Mexican pointed towards one of the pueblo's that was still standing and marched across the plaza with purpose.

"I guess we follow him," Zoe shrugged.

"Be careful, Zoe, I don't trust him," Maggie whispered huskily.

"Oh, he's harmless," Zoe waved her away, and half-jogged after the bandit.

Maggie growled, glancing nervously around at the deserted surroundings. It was a superb place to make someone disappear.

She squared her shoulders, retrieved the three black shoulder bags out of the back of the truck, and then strode after Zoe, keeping an eye out for intruders.

Maggie shivered as she entered the pueblo Marco and Zoe had disappeared into. It was dark and cold inside. She and Zoe stood aside as he used the shovel head to pry several rocks away from the base of a fire pit.

"It is under here," he mumbled, putting his back into upending a rather large boulder.

The boulder finally succumbed and Marco was able to pivot it a couple of feet away from the main cooking area. Maggie supposed that was what it was since there were numerous pieces of broken pottery around it.

Marco continued to shove aside debris, his shovel sparking whenever he hit a rock. The smell of singed rock, charcoal and loamy earth filled the air after twenty minutes of digging. The shovel banged against something solid. The hollow thud caused Marco to smile.

He bent down and wiped away the dirt from a weathered metal crate. Zoe and Maggie leaned forward, watching intently as he broke open the latches.

"You see, still here," Marco laughed, pulling out a fistful of American greenbacks.

"Oh, marvellous," Zoe clapped. "Now we'll be able to save Mary and Zoe."

"Si, marvellous," Marco echoed.

The grin that spread across his weathered and tanned face didn't reach his eyes, Maggie noticed.

"Do give Marco one of the bags," Zoe said surreptitiously.

Maggie swallowed a snarl and held out one of the bags. Marco let his fingers linger a moment too long on hers as he took the offered backpack from her.

"Oooh, let me get the shovel out of the way," Zoe trilled, fluttering around the hole in the ground like a hummingbird around a magnolia tree.

"Gracious," Marco beamed, reaching into the buried box to retrieve the thickly wrapped bundles of cash.

"I'm surprised Tommy left this much money here," Maggie said, marvelling at the sheer wealth buried beneath the hearth of this ancient pueblo.

"There used to be more, but Tommy gave a lot of it away to the church and to the orphanage where he grew up," Marco huffed, sweat running in rivulets down his face.

"Well, he gave some to you and your family too, I hope," Zoe gasped, her eyes glazing over, not with avarice, but with admiration.

"Senior Cortez paid me well," Marco growled, "but now he is just another preso in a gringo prison."

Maggie took a step back. The hatred that flashed briefly through Marco's eyes was palpable, but then it was gone as quickly as it came.

Marco filled the last of the bags with money.

Maggie went to lift one of the gym bags and staggered at its weight. She winced as she dragged it across the ground to the pueblo's sunken doorway. She couldn't wait to get away from this man.

There was a flicker of movement behind her. She turned swiftly and saw Marco grab for the shovel Zoe held in her hand, but Zoe was quicker. She hauled the shovel back and smashed it over his head. The bandit crumpled to the ground.

"You'll never get out of here," he rumbled as he fell to his knees. "My sons are out there. That money is my familia's now."

"No it is not," Zoe blazed, bringing the shovel down on Marco's head once again. "It's my fiancées."

Marco slammed face first into the ground.

"Zoe Puddicombe, I declare," Maggie marvelled.

"What? You think I don't know when a man has evil on his mind," Zoe quipped, brushing a hand across her spiky hair.

"Apparently," Maggie chuckled.

"Come on, let's get the bags in the truck," Zoe replied, perking up.

"You know they're really heavy. I wish you would have waited for Marco to load them into the back of the truck before you knocked him out cold," Maggie chimed.

"Oh well, too late now," Zoe grinned.

Maggie laughed as she dragged her bag across the piazza to the pickup truck. Behind her, Zoe gripped the bag and dragged it two handed across the dirt.

"How on earth did we ever get Cade into that wheelbarrow," Zoe snapped.

"We were a year younger then," Maggie joked.

The two women giggled like school girls as together they hoisted the two backpacks into the truck bed and then went to retrieve the last one.

"Do you think he was bluffing?" Zoe grunted, lifting up her side of the loot bag. "Do you think his sons are out there somewhere?"

"Well, if one of us gets shot that will answer the question," Maggie muttered through clenched teeth.

These gym bags were stupidly heavy. Who knew cash weighed that much.

The women tossed the last bag into the truck.

Something whizzed by Maggie's head. The sharp whine was followed by a hollow 'crack' as the bullet shattered a stone in the fountain's wall.

"Guess the boys are real," Zoe gasped.

"In the truck," Maggie commanded, racing for the driver's door.

Zoe hopped into the passenger side.

"Shit," Maggie swore.

"What?" Zoe demanded.

"I can't drive a stick shift, especially not one on the side of the wheel," Maggie cried, a lump rising into her throat.

"Oh, Hades, get out and run over here," Zoe spat. "I'll drive. Don't get shot!"

Maggie threw open the door, raced around the back of the truck, and then dived into the passenger seat, slamming the door shut as a couple more rifle shots bounced off the truck's hood and the stone wall behind it.

Zoe pounded her foot down on the clutch, slipped the truck into gear, and sped off in a hail of gravel.

"Zoe, you amaze me," Maggie grunted as a bullet glanced off the windshield. A crack suddenly appeared in the glass inches from Maggie's head.

"That's great, but where the heck are we going," she shouted, her hands white knuckling the steering wheel as the truck fishtailed up the steep road they came in on.

"We've been travelling south by south-east all day," Maggie answered. "At least, I think we have."

"So, north by north-west it is," Zoe agreed.

They topped the rise. Another rifle shot rang out. It hit the tailgate. Zoe swerved, but kept on driving, her foot to the floor.

"Drive, Zoe, drive," Maggie wailed.

"I am," Zoe hollered back.

Zoe raced across the desert in the pickup truck while Maggie swivelled in her seat to see if they were being followed yet. The only dust she saw was what they were kicking up.

"I don't see anyone," Maggie whispered.

"The boys must be checking on their father," Zoe nodded.

"Zoe, you're going in the wrong direction," Maggie hissed, realizing the truck was about to cross its own path. Zoe was driving in a circle.

"How am I supposed to know which way is north by north-west," Zoe demanded.

"That way," Maggie pointed. "Just keep the sun on your left shoulder."

"Fine," Zoe retorted.

"Fine," Maggie commented dryly.

They drove for another hour, Maggie continuously looking over her shoulder to monitor the desert behind them. It was strange that nobody seemed to be following them.

"Why aren't they following us," Zoe wondered aloud, glancing in the rear view mirror.

"I was just wondering the same thing," Maggie reaffirmed.

"You think they've bugged the truck," Zoe queried, her eyebrows shooting up.

"I don't think Marco is James Bond," Maggie snorted. "I think they think we don't know where we're going."

"Do we?" Zoe stammered. "Do we know where we're going?"

"How hard can it be to find the Rio Grande," Maggie insisted. "It's a mighty big river."

Zoe turned to stare at her friend, a look of complete disbelief on her face.

"Worse comes to worse, we'll ask the first person we see for directions," Maggie added. "I speak Spanish, un poco. My mother taught me, but it was so long ago, I barely remember how. Surely you must? Wasn't your last husband Spanish?"

"He was, but I never had to learn. I never dealt with the help," Zoe replied abstractly. "And his kids and I were rarely on speaking terms."

Maggie lifted her gaze from their back trail to the woman driving the pickup truck madly across the barely visible road across the desert. Maggie remained mute, thinking back to what Sylvie had recently advised her: think before you speak! Now was not the time to call Zoe out on her racist remarks. On the other hand, Zoe had agreed to marry Tommy Cortez. The woman beside her was a mass of contradictions.

Maggie turned back to the road ahead, searching for landmarks, her mind drifting as the road seemed to travel through a no man's land of rock, cactus, and dirt.

Zoe might be able to drive a stick shift, and she was handy with a shovel, but how on earth were the two of them going to get across the border in a stolen truck with three bags stuffed with cash in the back and no passports?

All at once, Maggie started to laugh. It started deep down in her belly and rolled upwards in a tidal wave of mirth.

"You want to be Thelma or Louise?" Maggie guffawed.

"Louise," Zoe grinned.

"Louise, it is," Maggie agreed, laughing even harder.

Zoe quickly joined in.

"I think I see a town up ahead," Zoe said, squinting into the sun. "Let's go steal another truck, preferably one without bullet holes."

Zoe and Maggie glanced at each other and burst into another fit of uncontrollable laughter.

Chapter Nineteen

You have to be secure enough to stand next to a stallion.
Keri Hilson

Gus, Dee, Sam and BJ rode side-by-side through the mining town.

Dee was pleased to see the two porta-potties in the back of the corral where she had instructed the race organizers to put them. She immediately cantered around the back of the hotel and reined to a halt in front of the outhouses.

"Awesome, too much coffee, I need a pee," the ranger grinned, brushing her hair from her face. She dismounted from her horse, the brawny little mustang she had ridden up the mountain the day before, and handed Gus the reins. Her roguishly handsome AFT lieutenant sat comfortably astride her rangy bay Quarter horse, a wide grin on his face.

"And there's toilet paper too," Gus laughed.

"There is," Dee giggled in return, disappearing into the john.

"I think I'll use the other one while we're here," Dee heard BJ say.

"You need me to hold your horse's reins?" Gus asked the teen.

"Nope," BJ replied.

Dee laughed. She could hear the humour in the teen's reply. His buckskin gelding was trained to ground tie, meaning the horse wouldn't move if the reins were loose and touching the ground.

"While you two are relieving yourselves, I'm gonna continue on up to the mine," Sam chortled.

Dee finished her business and emerged out of the outhouse. It was a glorious day. The sun was warm and bright. The birds were building nests. Even the robins had returned. The deer were already restless and preparing to return to the high country. That was fine by Dee. She hoped the cougars would stay in the mountains this year and away from the ranches. Once the deer headed up the slopes, it was pretty much guaranteed that the wolves and cougar would leave the ranches alone.

The big problem was it kept raining at night. It had rained early this morning as well so any tracks that may have helped them find the ladies would have been washed away.

"I hope the sheriff has better luck than we do," Gus whispered to Dee. BJ still didn't know about the kidnapping.

"Yeah, so far I haven't seen any signs of recent activity up here, not even animal tracks," Dee mumbled back, taking the mustang's reins back from her beau. "I don't think they came this way."

"Signs of what," BJ queried as he exited the porta-potty, picked up the buckskin's reins and swung effortlessly into the saddle.

"Issues with holding the race here," Dee returned smartly, hopping up onto the mustang.

"No, this is dope," BJ agreed. "I can't wait. Is it okay if I ride Bucky during the race or am I going to be manning a check-point?"

"I figure I'd get you to stay mounted. That way, if someone wanders off the trail, I can send you out to track them," Dee nodded as she swung her horse around.

"What about me," Gus grinned.

"You, I'm keeping close," Dee winked and kicked her horse into a light canter.

"She's the boss," Gus joked to BJ, spurring the gelding to catch up with the mustang.

BJ laughed outright and let his buckskin follow suit.

***

"Did you hear that?" Sylvie hissed, elbowing Mary. She eyed the gym junkie snoozing in the fold up chair across the narrow room.

"Hear what, the sound of my stomach growling?" Mary grumbled.

"I thought I heard something," Sylvie whispered fiercely. "I thought I heard horses and voices."

"Wishful thinking, my friend," Mary sighed wearily. "The cavalry aren't coming."

176

Three shadows flitted across the papered windows in the front of the building.

"Those are horses," Sylvie shouted. "I'm sure of it."

"Help," Mary screamed, sitting up straight.

"Help! Help us!" Sylvie joined in.

"Shut it," Percy yelled, jumping out of his chair. The camp chair toppled to the ground as he raced across the room, grabbed the rags he had forgotten to stuff back in the ladies mouths after lunch, and rammed them down their throats.

Sylvie tried to bite him, but was unsuccessful.

Even with a mouthful of rancid rag, she still tried to scream. All that came out was a muffled 'omphf'.

Damn it, she cursed. She should have screamed when she first thought she heard voices.

"You two yell like that again and I'll walk out of here and leave you to die, you got it," Adonis raged, shaking a fist in their faces. "Don't think I won't. I'm pretty freaked right now."

The muscled bozo's partner still hadn't shown up. She and Mary had been playing it up, ragging on Adonis that his partner wasn't coming back. The glazed look in his eyes and sunken rings around his eye sockets were tell tale signs. The kid was at the breaking point.

Sylvie forced herself to relax and stopped trying to break her bonds or make her kidnapper any madder. She was at the end of her endurance too. They hadn't eaten properly in three days now... or was it four? Sylvie wasn't sure.

Beside her, Mary looked as tired and hungry as she felt. Mary's skin was freakishly pale, her lips cracked and purple looking, and her silky hair greasy and plastered to the side of her face.

Yes, Adonis, might just leave them there to die if his buddy didn't show up soon. For the first time since they'd been snatched, Sylvie started praying for the punk rocker's return.

***

Zoe slowly edged the rusted canary yellow pickup truck into the solitary gas station with a single gas pump at the end of the main street of a strange little town. The streets and structures appeared to be haphazardly arranged. There was a cantina and a tiny grocery store with bins of fruit and vegetables out front. Broken down trucks, cars and garbage littered the yards of the houses she could see.

"This is a sad little place," Zoe gulped.

"No esperanza here," Maggie agreed.

A lithe pretty girl of about sixteen with short cropped hair, angel tattoos on her arms, a silver cross fastened on a leather thong around her neck, hoop earrings, and a nose ring, sauntered out of the building as they pulled up to the pumps.

"You ladies lost," the girl said, breaking into a broad grin.

"Oh, good, you speak English," Zoe smiled through the open window. "Which way to the border?"

The girl eyed the three bags in the back of the truck.

178

"No, no," she frowned, waving them away. "Go away. I can't help you."

"Look, we don't need help, just directions," Zoe continued.

"She knows that, Zoe," Maggie sighed. "She also knows who we are. That is why nobody is following us. I bet Senior Coyote owns this desperate little town."

"And how could she know that?" Zoe quipped. "I don't believe it."

"Oh, I don't know, maybe the bullet holes in the truck," Maggie snapped.

"Everyone knows who you are, lady," the girl shrugged, pushing away from the window.

"Can't you just lift one finger and point," Zoe grunted, her gaze fixed upon the teen as she walked around the other side of the truck. "Come on, don't you love your grandma? We're grandmas too. We just want to get home to see our grandkids."

The girl chewed her lip for a minute, undecided.

Maggie once again held her tongue.

Grandmas? Grandkids? Neither of them looked like a grandma!

"My grandma's a drunk," the girl smirked.

Zoe huffed in disappointment.

"And neither of you ladies look like grandma material," the teen quipped.

"She's got us there," Zoe shrugged.

"How much," Maggie asked the girl standing beside the gas pump.

"One of those bags in the back of the truck will do it," the teen smiled crookedly.

"Do you really want to go there, little girl," Maggie sneered, pulling two one hundred dollar bills out of her wallet. "After all, you know who is after us."

The girl rolled her eyes and snapped the bills out of Maggie's hand.

"That way," she snickered, pointing towards the road on the right. She tucked the bills into her pant's pocket. "Keep going until you hit the highway."

Maggie nodded thanks as Zoe put the truck into gear and pulled out of the gas station.

"Think we can trust her?" Zoe asked.

"Doubt it," Maggie noted.

A rifle shot rang out. Another bullet tore through the tailgate.

"Floor it," Maggie screamed as more bullets hit the back of the truck.

"Criminy, what is wrong with these people?" Zoe yelled, fishtailing onto the road the girl had indicated.

Maggie glanced backwards. Once again, nobody was following them. She paled. This was not good!

Chapter Twenty

The hardest thing about learning to ride is the ground.

Sam hung his head down as they rode out of the forest and into the pullout at the highway's edge which marked the end of the upcoming race course. He felt like a gopher was tunnelling a hole through his gut.

It was about three o'clock in the afternoon and he was tired. The lack of sleep was catching up to him. He hoped Emma would be able to get some shut eye while he and BJ were gone.

The ride was spectacular, but there were no tracks or any indication that anyone had been driving up in the hills either in a four-by-four or an all terrain vehicle. It was a slim chance anyway.

Sam and Cole were pretty sure that the kidnappers were holding the ladies in a remote house or abandoned building somewhere close to the prison. Cole had his men checking on those sites now.

The mine and the mining town were all empty, the mine itself and the heritage buildings too dangerous to enter.

Sam hated the idea of facing Emma with no leads to go on. He was taking all this hard, but Emma was truly distraught. The fact his daughter-in-law was able to function at all around the kids was a miracle.

"I'll load up Checkers and take you to pick up your truck, Dee," Sam offered, dismounting in front of his Chevy truck and stock trailer. "You can drive back to pick up Gus and the horses."

"That's okay, Sam, we'll ride back to the truck along the highway," Gus jumped in. "Maybe Dee and I can spot a set of tracks that seems unusual."

"Good idea," Sam agreed. It was hard to think clearly. He was happy Gus was here, despite his earlier misgivings.

"Is there something you're not telling me," BJ asked, his blue eyes flashing as he dismounted his horse. "You guys have been weird all day."

Sam, Gus, and Dee, exchanged a wary look.

Sam sighed. BJ was fifteen. Sam had to remind himself regularly his grandson wasn't a kid anymore.

"I'm sorry, but your mother and I didn't quite tell you and Jenny the truth, son," Sam said, letting out a long breath.

"We didn't want to freak your sister out," Gus added.

"Sylvie and Mary were kidnapped," Sam continued. "The kidnappers thought one of them was Mr Cortez's fiancée. The kidnappers don't know they've got the wrong women."

"Needless to say, we have to keep that fact a secret," Gus said.

"That's why you came with me and Dee, Grandpa, to look for signs of the kidnappers," BJ queried. "And that's why you're here too, isn't it Gus?"

"Yes," Sam nodded. "It was a long shot, but you can see a lot of country from atop those ridges."

"What about Miss Zoe and Miss Carroll? Please don't tell me they're missing too?" BJ begged them, his face reddening.

"They aren't," Sam reassured the teen. "They've gone to pick up the ransom money."

Sam refrained from telling the boy they were in Mexico. He was still angry about that. Tommy's son, JJ, or Sam, should have gone to get the money, despite the risks. He was still angry with himself for not tagging along with them.

"I don't mind riding along with Dee and Gus. I want to help," BJ stuttered.

"Right now, I need you at the ranch more than ever," Sam quaked. "I don't want your mother handling those studs with only Jenny there, especially that knot head of Maggie's."

"Okay," BJ said, crestfallen. "I understand."

"And I still want you with me on race day," Dee consoled him. "It's going to be tough to keep an eye on all the entrants and watch out for anything fishy going on if we haven't found the ladies by then."

"Yes, ma'am," BJ nodded, leading his Quarter horse into the trailer.

"Thank you both," Sam said, his deep voice cracking.

"We'll find them, Sam," Gus reiterated, nodding encouragement. "Those are two tough old broads. I pity the kidnappers."

Sam chuckled despite his misgivings. They were strong women, Gus was right about that.

"I'll talk to you tomorrow," Sam said, tipping his hat to the ranger and ATF lieutenant. He then loaded his mare into the trailer.

It was good to have friends like Cole, Dee and Gus.

***

Benny slowed down on the highway. He was about to pull into the turn off leading to the mining town, but there was a three quarter ton pickup truck with a horse trailer in his way.

"Damn," he swore, swerving back onto the highway.

He continued down the highway, passing yet another pickup truck and horse trailer with four people, two on the ground holding horses, and two in the saddle, beside it. Benny cruised on by without turning his head to stare.

"At least they don't look like cops," he groaned as he continued down the highway.

Benny glanced at the bucket of chicken legs and French fries on the seat beside him. A cardboard cup holder with four cups of coffee in it sat on the floor of the Bronco.

"May as well eat," he muttered and turned up the volume on the hard rock station on the radio. There was a truck stop a few miles ahead. He could wait there for the horseback riders to go home. If Percy and the broads had to eat cold chicken and fries it was no skin off his nose.

***

Emma sat on the porch with a cup of Earl Grey tea, a toothy smile on her face as she listened to Jenny singing to Mike. Her daughter was currently interlacing pink, blue, and yellow ribbons in the donkey's wispy mane and tale. The donkey's eyes were closed. The old guy didn't seem to mind.

"Why all the different colour of ribbons today, sweetie," she asked her daughter.

"Cause the race is only a few days away and I want to focus on our training," Jenny squeaked. "I've been reading about how the Olympic riders train and they say you got to stay focused. This way, I don't have to ribbon Mike up on race day. I just got to focus like Baby Yoda does when he tries to unleash the Force."

"Yes, but why pink, yellow and blue," Emma grinned.

"That's so I can pick Mike out in a crowd," she nodded sagely. "There's gonna be a lot of donkeys there."

Emma smothered a laugh. She doubted there were going to be many one eared donkeys in the race, but she didn't want to spoil Jenny's fun.

"I hope my cowgirl grandmas are all back for the race," Jenny twittered, looking up from her braiding.

"I hope so too, sweetie," Emma mumbled.

***

185

The truck let out a rumbling cough and glided to a stop on the country road. A cloud of dust drifted into the cab through the open windows. Maggie and Zoe wheezed, covering their mouths with a tissue.

Zoe tried to restart the truck, but the starter gave out after two unsuccessful attempts.

"What do you think it is," Maggie gasped.

"How should I know I'm not a mechanic?"

"Maybe we ran out of gas," Maggie suggested, annoyed.

Zoe glanced at the gas gage. It was on empty, but didn't gas gages always read empty when the vehicle wasn't running? She had never thought to look before.

"What do you think we should do?" Zoe moaned. "We're in the middle of nowhere with a bunch of crazed goons after us."

Maggie gave her an odd look and popped open the door.

Ugh, Zoe thought, pursing her lips, *that woman was so annoying*.

Zoe pushed open her own door. It squeaked on rusty hinges. She got out of the truck and stretched. Her lower back and right calve muscle were screaming. She found it hard to breathe. The heat was excruciating, the dust burning her throat and lungs. They had drunk the last of their water hours ago. She dabbed the sweat from her face with a makeup pad. She must look ghastly.

Keep a stiff upper lip, her mother used to tell her. Her mother was British. Etiquette was everything.

Zoe brushed her fingers through her gritty hair and put on a bright smile.

"Do you think we can drag those bags of money with us if we have to walk?" Zoe asked her partner in crime.

"Not very far in this heat," Maggie sighed, wiping the dirt from her neck with a tissue.

"Point taken," Zoe agreed. "We are in a pickle, Thelma."

"We are that, Louise," Maggie smiled grimly.

"Well, I have to pee," Zoe announced. "I'm going to go potty down by that copse of bushes over there."

"Watch out for snakes," Maggie replied with a shake of her head. "I'm not sucking rattlesnake venom out of your bottom."

"Don't be so dramatic," Zoe waved as she strutted over to the copse of trees some fifty feet from the truck, a wide grin on her face. The image of Maggie bending over to kiss her butt was hilarious.

Maggie was right about the snakes though. Zoe crept through the bushes, found an appropriate spot and pulled down her jeans. Her nerves twitched. The hair on her arms stood to attention as she tinkled. It felt like someone was watching her.

Zoe quickly finished her whiz, yanked up her pants and looked around. Two big wet round eyes regarded her from the shade of the bushes. It was a calf, not newly born, but close to it.

"Ohhh, look at you," she cried. "Aren't you gorgeous?" She reached out to touch the calf when she heard a bellow. Zoe swung around. An enormous long horned cow snorted in anger. Momma bellowed once again and crashed through the brush towards her. Zoe raced back to the truck.

"Get in the truck," she screamed.

Maggie turned towards her. The color drained from her face.

"Move," Zoe shouted again.

Maggie jumped into the truck, slammed the door shut, and quickly rolled up her window as Zoe staggered, falling against the hood, righted herself, and jumped into the driver's seat. The cow circled the truck, stomping her hooves and raging at the woman who had disturbed her calf.

"I think I pulled my groin," Zoe whimpered.

"I thought you were a goner," Maggie drawled, her brown eyes fixed upon the irate long horn. "I couldn't have run that fast."

"Well, I am younger than you," Zoe murmured, perking up, despite the pain that ripped through her knees and groin.

"No you're not," Maggie hissed.

Maggie rolled her window down a couple of inches.

"It's sweltering in here, and that cow stinks," she continued, wrinkling her nose.

Maggie was right. Heat waves shimmered across the truck's hood and along the road. Even a few minutes with the windows rolled up were suffocating.

"Look, she's going back to her calf," Zoe pointed, relief flooding through her.

"No more peeing in the bushes, Louise," Maggie chuckled.

"Agreed, Thelma," Zoe grinned.

They rolled the windows down once momma disappeared from view.

Why on earth had she agreed to come on this foolhardy journey? Neither Sylvie nor Mary was her friend. She lived with them, and liked them, but they only just met a year ago. Of course, there was the matter of Zoe's sleeping with Sylvie's husband, but what of it?

Perhaps it was misplaced quilt?

That was probably it, Zoe sighed. If this situation ever happened again, she vowed to stay at home. She didn't want to be the one holding the short end of the stick like she appeared to be doing now.

Chapter Twenty-One

A mule is just like horse, but even more so.

Emma paced about the kitchen, her stomach in turmoil. JJ had called. The ladies didn't show. He was going to stay near the tunnel entrance for as long as he could without attracting the attention of the border patrol.

Had it all been a setup? Was Zoe and Maggie alive or were they being tortured by the cartel? JJ seemed convinced that something minor had happened to delay them.

They had been gone for over twenty-four hours. The worst imaginable things were somersaulting through Emma's mind.

It was the Lord's Day.

After Sam and BJ finished with the horses, she would pack the family up and head to church. A little fire and brimstone was just what she needed to renew her faith and calm her fears.

She looked out the window. The boys were releasing the last of the stallions in their paddocks and Jenny was dragging Mike up the lane in her never ending quest to get the donkey to jog, the two Saint Bernards running laps around them. The rainbow of ribbons in Mike's mane and tail fluttered in the breeze.

Cole's Suburban turned up their drive. He slowed and waved to Jenny, and then continued on up to the house. He parked the vehicle, waving to Sam and BJ in the fields as he stepped out of the SUV.

Emma prayed Cole had some good news to share.

"Cole, tell me you've made progress," she stammered. Cole kissed her on the cheek. He smelled of Ivory soap and Polo aftershave.

"Not yet," he sighed, hat in hand. "We're not giving up though and I don't want you to either."

"You're reading my mind again," she cried, wrapping her arms around him.

"That's not hard to do," he murmured in her ear. "We've covered a lot of ground but there are still a few places left to check. The warden and I are sure one of the inmates at the prison orchestrated this. Cortez agrees and has feelers out. If we can identify the inmate involved, we'll have a better handle on where to search."

"I'm praying every day for the safe return of our friends," Emma wept.

"Look, I know this has shaken you, but we'll find them," Cole told her, hugging her even more fiercely.

Emma was angry with herself for being so weak. It wasn't like her. She had kept it together when Cleve was killed in Iraq, worked tirelessly to make *The Silver Spurs Home for Aging Cowgirls* a success, helped hunt down a mountain lion, and raised two amazing kids. She could handle this.

"I promise you we'll find them, alive and well," Cole whispered fiercely.

"Don't make promises you can't keep," Emma trembled. The words stung. They were so similar to the last words Cleve had said to her before he died overseas serving his country: *I promise you I'll return, alive and well.*

Cole didn't know about Zoe and Maggie's trip to Mexico to pick up three million dollars in ill gotten gains and the lack of delivery thereof. Emma didn't want to go there. It would put Cole in a ridiculously bad predicament and she didn't want to think about how horrible it would be to lose all of the ladies she had become so attached to.

She had become terribly attached to all of the ladies, she realized. She loved them in fact. No matter what they did in the past, the four crazy old horsewomen were family.

***

Percy yawned and stretched as he ushered the ladies out to the outhouses. He had to admit he was worried about the old girls. Their hair was limp, their eyes red rimmed, and they dragged their feet as they walked across the sandy corral. He had taken to tying their hands in front of them instead of behind them to at least give them some sense of dignity, plus he swore he was never going to wipe another person's bum as long as he lived.

Benny had shown up in the dead of night with a bucket of cold fried chicken and greasy French fries. At least the coffee he brought was fresh. His partner was supposed to bring everyone Egg McMuffins for breakfast but 'seeing is believing' as they say. So far, Benny wasn't proving to be very reliable.

As Percy waited for the ladies to finish their business, he noticed there were a bunch of orange ribbons fluttering in the breeze along the road. There were lots more horse tracks too. He must be losing it. He hadn't heard anything. How could so many riders pass the hotel without him hearing anything?

Today was supposed to be payday. After today, it would all be over. He'd go to Canada and find someplace to open up a gym. Mexico was out of the question. Percy had no doubt Cortez would find him if he was dumb enough to go there. Soon, the ladies could go home, have a hot bath, real food, and sleep in their own beds, and he'd be rid of Benny.

Mary and Sylvie felt like comrades in arms. Last night changed everything. The gals were right about Benny: Benny was out for Benny.

"Please tell me it ain't granola bars for breakfast again," Sylvie growled as she exited the outhouse and shuffled back to the hotel.

"Ditto," Mary mumbled as she walked by.

"I hear ya," Percy agreed. "Today's the last day though. I'll make sure you gals will be okay."

"Yeah, well, don't be surprised if that partner of yours hangs you out to dry and leaves you empty handed," Sylvie warned him.

"Nah, Benny's a jerk, but we've been friends since we were kids," Percy admonished her.

"Sweetie, you're a good boy, just plumb naïve," Mary quipped.

Percy didn't respond as he opened the door for the ladies.

Benny wouldn't do that, would he?

As he was about to close the door, Benny pulled in with breakfast. The sight of his buddy made him feel better, until he saw the white knuckles holding the McDonald's bag and blazing brown eyes.

"This place is like Grand Central Station," he seethed. "Have you seen all the horse tracks?"

"Not really," Percy shrugged. "Nobody found us."

Benny glared at him, tossed the bag with the McDonald's muffins in it into the air, spun on his heel and headed back to the Bronco.

Percy snatched the bag out of the air.

"Stay out'a sight, I'll be back to get you when I got the cash," he yelled, slamming the truck's door, and spinning out of the yard.

"I guess there's no coffee then," Percy mumbled. "The gals won't be happy."

***

Maggie awoke with a crick in her neck. She heard a tap-tapping on the window and shuddered as two large looming shapes leaned towards her.

"Senioritas, you okay," a round faced boy asked.

The boy was joined by another round faced teen of about eleven years-old. They stood beside the truck eating tamales. Their faces were tanned and pleasant, their eyes wide with concern, smiles tickling their lips at such a wonderful early morning find. Behind them stood a mule and a burro.

"Good morning," Maggie replied cheerfully, her stomach grumbling at the smell of the spicy food.

"Oh, hello," Zoe murmured, rubbing the sleep from her eyes. "Where did you come from?"

"The hacienda," the shorter of the boys said, pointing west past where the momma big horn cow and her calf had been.

"I don't suppose you have any more of those scrumptious smelling tamales," Maggie purred, turning on the charm.

The boys nodded and walked over to their mounts. Both the mule and the burro were on the small side, but stout beasts all the same. The mule was an ebony coloured bay with a light muzzle and the donkey was storm cloud grey with a silver muzzle.

The boys retrieved a couple of paper wrapped parcels and brought them back to the truck.

"Fifty Pesos each," said the taller boy.

"That's highway robbery! Would you do that to your grandmother if she was stranded in the desert?" Zoe persisted once again.

"My grandmother would charge double," the shorter boy laughed.

Maggie groaned and pushed open her door. Zoe needed another story line.

"I'll tell you what," Maggie grinned, reaching into the truck bed and unzipping a bag. She pulled out two stacks of one hundred dollar bills. She guessed there were one hundred of the one hundred dollar bills in each stack, making it ten thousand dollars per bundle. The boys' faces lit up.

"I'll give you one packet each for the tamales, a canteen of water, any other food you have, and both of those fine animals," Maggie said, putting on her best negotiator's face.

"I can't sell the mule, Seniorita, he's not mine," the taller boy groaned.

The other boy smacked him on the arm.

Maggie smothered a laugh, reached back in the bag, and pulled out one more stack of cash.

"That's my final offer!"

The boys grinned, handed Maggie the pastry in their hands, and raced back to their mounts.

Maggie handed a pastry to Zoe. Zoe eyed the giant tamale with trepidation until hunger got the better of her. Her eyes watered as she took a bite of it and swallowed.

Maggie laughed.

"We'll leave the canteen on the saddle," the taller boy said, stuffing the cash into one of the burro's saddle bags.

"Si, mine too," said the other, handing Maggie the mule and burro's reins.

The boys skipped off down the road, elbowing each other and whooping with glee at the handfuls of cash they carried.

"You paid way too much for those beasts," Zoe mumbled through a mouth full of pastry.

"Who cares? It' not our money," Maggie beamed.

"That's true, and those boys were certainly adorable," Zoe winked from the driver's seat.

"Hey, lady, my mule bucks," the taller boy shouted, a wicked grin on his face.

"You can have that one," Zoe giggled.

After they ate and took a few swigs of hot metallic water from the canteens, they tied the bags of money to the back of the saddles. The mule carried two bags since Zoe and the one bag of cash was more than enough for the straggly burro.

"I think I'll call him, Cade," Maggie said, eyeing the ebony mule. The last thing she needed was a broken hip, but she was not about to walk to the border leading the mule just because it had a temper. "Seems appropriate given I rode him for years and he was as obstinate as I expect this mule to be."

"And I'll call mine O'Hara," Zoe announced.

Zoe hopped swung a leg over the burro. O'Hara let out a short bray in protest. She waited for something to happen, but the placid burro simply licked his lips and wandered over to munch on some grass beside the road. Zoe sagged with relief, picked up the reins, and clucked to the burro.

Maggie braced herself and reached for the saddle horn. The mule pinned back its ears and lifted a leg. Maggie instantly removed her foot from the stirrup, lengthened the reins and drove the mule away from her using the reins as a crop. The mule tried to side kick her, but she booted him lightly in the rear end and yanked his head towards her.

"I'll have none of that, Cade," Maggie growled.

She continued to drive him in a circle until the mule pricked his ears forward and licked his lips in supplication.

"Good boy," she said, putting a boot back in the stirrup and hauling her leg over the bags of loot before slipping the other foot into the stirrup.

"He sure is boney."

"Maybe you better think of another name," Zoe joked. "Cade was anything but."

Maggie snickered and urged the mule forward.

"He's got the same attitude as Desert Storm," Maggie noted.

Zoe kicked her burro, asking for more speed, but it didn't happen. The burro plodded along after Maggie's mule with his head down and eyes half closed.

"I give up," Zoe moaned in frustration.

"Just remember a mule never forgets. I expect a burro doesn't either," Maggie chuckled. "Be nice to O'Hara."

"His legs are so short he's a surprisingly smooth ride. If I flex my toes, I can almost touch the ground. Cade looks like a rough ride," Zoe quipped.

"He always was, darling," Maggie grinned.

The ladies rode all day, stopping a couple of times to give the animals some water and a much needed rest. It was obvious they were getting closer to the river as the grass grew longer and greener, and the air a little cooler.

By the time they got to the highway, all four of them were tired and grumpy.

They sat upon their mounts on a ridge, staring down at the muddy water of the Rio Grande and the constant stream of car and truck traffic heading to the border crossing.

"I think we should cross the highway at night," Zoe shouted over the din of the traffic.

"Good idea, let's go back to that copse of trees and unsaddle these guys. We can all use a break," Maggie yelled back.

Zoe nodded and they turned back, letting the animals pick their way down the rocky trail to the gully they had just emerged from.

***

Bruce watched warily as Tommy sat down amidst a group of cartel members, casually throwing a leg over the bench seat beside the leader as if it was just another day at the office. He wanted to sit closer to the table to hear what was being said but didn't dare. There were tables of affiliated gang members and bikers all around them.

A knot formed in his stomach. The back of his neck felt like an iron rod had been shoved down his spine. There was no news from Benny. Bruce had sat in the yard all day, hoping to catch the flash of lights from his son's Bronco. So far, it was a zilch.

Something must have happened in Mexico. Why else would Tommy be sitting with the cartel boys?

Bruce prayed Benny wouldn't panic. His kid was long on temper and short on brains. Killing Tommy's fiancée wasn't an option, not yet anyway. Tommy might insist on 'proof of life'.

The old inmate slipped away, trying to remain calm, despite how badly frayed his nerves were at that moment. If he hurried, he could get to the library in time. He needed to type something up quick, and slip the note under Tommy's pillow before he returned to the cell. He didn't want to be there when Tommy read the new note. After he that, he'd run to the shower room and throw-up.

***

Tommy returned to his cell. He was livid. The cartel boys had informed him that Marco had reopened Tommy's delinquent tunnels and undercut their people. It was news to Tommy. He had assured them he would take care of it.

When JJ hadn't called him by dinner time, he knew there was trouble. If anything happened to his women, he'd call in every favour he could to escape and go back to Mexico to find them.

Park wasn't there. An envelope was stuffed hastily under his pillow once again.

"You screwed up. No drop. No wedding. You have 72 hours. In 48 hours, details on where to drop the cash will be provided." That was the entire note.

Tommy punched his pillow. He wanted to let loose, but going berserk would only get him tossed into solitary.

Park skidded to a stop when he saw Tommy.

Tommy reined in his fury. He could smell the sickly stench of fear on his cellmate. Park's face looked green.

"You okay, Tommy," Park asked.

"I'm fine, just fine, amigo," Tommy smiled, his mood lightening as his cellmate visibly paled.

So, it was the fat man all along! Was it a big surprise? Not really. The gelatinous leech was just smart enough to pull this off and foolish enough to think he could get away with it.

"Hey, you know that guy you asked me get a bead on," Bruce stuttered. "Well, he got released today. He got out on good behaviour. I only got his first name though, it's Wally."

"Good to know," Tommy nodded, the wheels turning on how to handle this… maybe bring him into the loop by making Park think he was part of Tommy's inner circle.

"You know, I was thinking," the former America's Most Wanted felon grinned, "I got something maybe you can help me with."

His cellmate nodded like a bubble headed doll.

Chapter Twenty-Two

"Now I'm a flyin', talkin' donkey! You might seen a housefly. Maybe even a superfly. But I bet you ain't never seen a donkey fly!"

Donkey, Shrek

Maggie and Zoe rode along the trail beside the wide rushing river beneath the pale moonlight. The night was crisp and clear. It was a relief to get away from the simmering heat, but now that night had fallen, so too had the temperature.

The river raged beside the trail. They could hear the rustle of critters in the bushes beside the trail above the rushing of water over stone.

They could see the border wall, a black monolith stretching from horizon to horizon. It was so obsidian that even the moonlight didn't reflect off of it.

Voices travelled at night. Despite the noise from the river and the night things, several times they had to stop and hide from the border patrol and Mexican police. Even worse than that were the coyotes running hopeful immigrants across the border. The possibility of getting shot was increasing by the minute.

"Maggie, I'm freezing," Zoe whined from atop the burro named O'Hara. "My fingers and feet are numb."

"Me too," Maggie stuttered, her teeth chattering.

"Do we have anything to make a fire with," Zoe croaked.

"I don't think so, but we can't anyway. It's too dangerous. I see a light up ahead. It looks like a church," Maggie whispered. A white steeple rose like a ghost in the night. "Maybe we can hide in there for awhile."

"Good idea," Zoe hissed.

Zoe hunched over her burro, trying to absorb as much heat as she could. Maggie sympathized. She had wrapped her hands in Cade's mane to keep her fingers warm.

The two ladies rode up to the church. There was a single light glowing inside the church's stained glass windows and the flicker from a hundred candles. A stained glass window featuring the Mother Mary and Baby Jesus watched the two of them dismount.

"I'll see if it's open, you stay with the animals," Maggie croaked, her voice muffled.

Maggie climbed the steps and grabbed hold of the door handle. She yanked on the handle and the door popped open. Candles lined the church's bye-alter and the dais in front of a statue of Mother Mary. Maggie's cheeks burned as the warm air hit her. The church smelled of lemon oil and burning wax.

"Ola, can I help you," a deep baritone voice echoed through the expanse.

"I'm sorry, I didn't see you there," Maggie squinted into the darkened rectory where a priest sat at a desk reading the bible by candle light.

"Our Lady of Grace is open twenty-four hours," the pastor nodded, his presence both friendly and majestic in his black robes and white collar.

"My friend and I are trying to get back home," Maggie stammered, at a loss for words. She didn't want to lie to a priest.

"And would that be the woman out there holding onto the mule and the burro," the pastor grinned.

"It would," Maggie shrugged sheepishly.

"You look tired," he said. "You are safe here. We are a sanctuary for those on the run or looking for a new life. You may release the mule and burro in the cemetery out back. It is gated and the weeds need a good trimming. I don't think the dead will mind."

The priest's laugh was music to Maggie's ears; finally, a friend and ally.

"Thank you, we could use a respite," she nodded.

Maggie went to inform Zoe of their luck and to help unsaddle the animals. The two of them then dragged the money bags into the chapel, tucking them out of the way in a coat closet.

"Oh, thank God, heat," Zoe exclaimed with relief. "I'm a popsicle. Oops, sorry, pastor."

"I am sure God has heard worse," the priest mused, his brown eyes sparkling.

"Come, I have hot cocoa and cookies in the rectory," the pastor motioned towards the curtains behind his desk where a door stood open. "My wife made the cookies this morning."

Maggie and Zoe retreated to the rectory with the pastor, glad of the warmth and the pastor's aid. It seemed the church was a major stop on the search for a better world.

"If you want, I have someone I trust who can slip you across the border," the pastor offered after the gals had their fill of chocolate and sugar cookies.

"I don't know," Maggie replied thoughtfully. "There are some really bad guys after us. I'm not sure we should have even stopped here. We've put you in incredible danger, padre."

"And what about Cade and O'Hara," Zoe cried.

"Who is Cade and O'Hara? I didn't see anyone else with you?"

"Our delightfully cranky mounts," Maggie replied.

"I am sure I can find someone to take them," the pastor chuckled, resting his chin in his hands as he leaned on the table.

"Mags, we can't let them end up at the knackers," Zoe worried. "I've become rather fond of O'Hara."

Maggie shook her head. Leave it to Zoe to fall in love with a pesky burro. Cade had a rather bad temperament, but a full belly might soften his temper, Maggie reasoned. She had to admit, she didn't want to see him end up in a slaughterhouse either. It wasn't the mule or burro's fault they were now homeless. It was hers.

"I have to agree with my friend," Maggie sighed. "We need to keep going. I think we're safer on our own. Nobody will expect two old women on a mule and a burro of being anything but two old women on a mule and a burro. We appreciate what you've already done for us."

"Then at least let me get you some warm ponchos and gloves," the pastor said, standing up.

"We won't say 'no' to that," Zoe remarked, her sunburned face glowing.

"If you continue to ride up river, you will come across an ancient river crossing. There used to be a rope ferry there. A hundred paces from the crossing, it gets very shallow and you should be able to ride across it. That is all I can help you with," the priest continued, offering them each woollen ponchos and hand knitted mittens. "I don't know where you can cross the wall. You may have to ride many miles for that. Watch out for the drones too. Both sides use those now."

Maggie and Zoe hugged the Father. It was unusual for Maggie to want to hug a priest, but the broad shouldered grey haired pastor was different. There was an air of 'goodness' around him that couldn't be faked.

Maggie stopped on the way out and opened up one of the sacks. She took six bundles of hundred dollar bills out of it and stuffed them inside the collection box. She didn't care if Tommy approved or not. The kidnappers would have to suck it up too. She had never counted how much they had in each pack. She only knew it was a lot of moola.

The mule and burro seemed happier for the rest and the lush grass in the cemetery. Cade even nickered to her when she approached him with the saddle.

***

"I feel like a bandit," Zoe joked as they arrived at the rotting poles and moss covered ropes of the old ferry crossing. The ferry itself was a sunken wreck of broken boards, the sorrowful remains wedged into the sandy banks of the river. "All I need is a fedora."

Maggie chortled.

Zoe could see the back of the raven haired woman in the red, white and black poncho, riding the equally raven haired mule ahead of her. Her silhouette was accentuated by the lightening sky as the stars folded in upon themselves and the moon sank below the horizon. The rising sun was a bright red ball.

"There's the crossing the pastor talked about," Maggie pointed. "Look, the river isn't so fast over there."

"I see it," Zoe remarked, leaning sideways to peek around Maggie's solid form.

They rode up to the sandy bank and stared down at the wide river.

"Well, let's hope it is safe," Maggie braced herself and kicked Cade into the water.

The mule stopped for a quick drink. Maggie let him so Zoe did the same with O'Hara. As soon as the bay lifted his head, Maggie urged him forward.

The current was stronger than it looked. Zoe's burro stumbled; water sloshed over Zoe's boots and soaked her jeans to the top of her thighs. The burro was shorter than Maggie's mule, the water up to his belly.

"Slow down, Mags, O'Hara's isn't as tall as Cade," Zoe cried.

"I can't stop now," Maggie shouted from the middle of the river. "Keep going and prepare to bale if you need to."

Zoe cringed. She wasn't a good swimmer.

"Come on, O'Hara, you can do it," she urged her mount, leaning forward over the saddle horn to place more weight on his shoulder.

Oh dear, perhaps I should have leaned backwards, Zoe chastised herself. *The little things she had taken for granted were getting so hard to remember.*

The burro stumbled hard, crumpling at the knees, its face going under the water. Zoe screamed. Only the burro's ears were visible above the water line. She leaned back, kicking her feet out of the stirrups in case he rolled over, but the hardy animal lunged forward and into shallower water, its sad face dripping wet.

"You okay," Maggie hollered as her mule leapt up the bank on the far side of the river.

"I'm okay," Zoe waved, patting her burro affectionately.

Zoe breached the shore and climbed out of the river, her feet dangling below the stirrups. In truth, she didn't use them much, they were too short, the leathers not long enough to buckle any lower.

"Who's a good boy," she crooned, hugging the beast around the neck.

"I think he's smiling," Maggie laughed, swivelling in her saddle.

A bullet whizzed by Zoe's head. The animals reared and bolted. Both Maggie and Zoe held on tight, letting their mounts have their heads as they galloped up the rocky slope to the top of the hill. The steel barrier blocked their escape, forcing them to veer east away from the armed guards at the border crossing.

Zoe heard an ATV on the far side of the river.

"Down there, into those trees," Maggie yelled.

Zoe galloped on, the burro's eggbeater gait hammering her spine into submission. She wasn't sure how much punishment her back could take. Ahead of her, Maggie wasn't faring much better, Cade's gait launching her out of the saddle with every stride.

Maggie turned sharply on the slope, letting the sure footed mule pick its way around the rocks, its rear end sliding down the slope. There was a deer trail at the bottom of the grade that headed into the trees. It was just wide enough for the slim burro and mule.

"Do you think we lost them?" Zoe stuttered, her voice mirroring her terror.

"For now, but we have to keep going," Maggie insisted. "You didn't lose any of the money in the river, did you?"

"No," Zoe said, reaching behind her. Luck was with them. The bag of cash was still fastened to the saddle, but it was as sodden as she and the burro were. She hoped she didn't get blisters from riding in wet clothes.

***

"Mom, Grandpa," Jenny asked, holding a spoonful of Cheerios in the air. "Since tomorrow's a ProD day for the teachers, can I take Mike up the race trail with BJ. I'd rather find out now if he can do it rather than on race day in front of all of my friends."

209

"That's probably a good idea, honey, but I'm not sure you should," Emma said, offering Sam a questioning look. "It's not fair to everyone else, is it?"

"I don't mind," BJ mouthed through a mouthful of toast. "I can ride Patch. He could use a bit of light exercise. The dogs could come too. The Dozer will keep us safe."

Emma didn't seem mollified, but Sam couldn't see how it would hurt. Maybe he'd ride along with them. It would be better than sitting around the ranch stewing.

"How about I call Dee and ask her," Sam grinned. "She is the boss. If it is okay, we can make a family day out of it. We'll take Checkers and Penny too."

"Oh, and leave Bucky in the pasture to keep the studs quiet," BJ grinned back.

"I don't know if that's a good idea," Emma stammered.

"You're right, Em," Sam nodded. "We'll put the studs and filly in the back paddocks where they can't get into any trouble while we're gone. We'll leave them out today as long as possible."

"Yay!" Jenny hollered with joy, leaping to her feet to race around the kitchen table to hug her grandfather and mother in turn.

"That's only if Dee agrees, sweetheart," Sam laughed.

"She will," Jenny quipped. "Ranger Dee loves Mike. She won't want him to embarrass himself either.

"Alright, I'll go too, but only if you hustle it and get down to the bus stop lickety-split or you'll miss the school bus," Emma laughed.

Sam's heart melted as his grandkids kissed their mother goodbye and raced out of the door to catch the school bus.

Chapter Twenty-Three

Whinnying is everything!

"Quick, they're onto us," Zoe yelped. Behind her a six pack of tough looking brutes ran up the river bank towards them, rifles slung over their shoulders.

"This way, the fence has been cut," Maggie yelled, spurring her mule on.

Zoe whacked her burro on the rump with a length of rein. She felt horrid about it, but worse about being caught now.

She grinned when her burro raced through the opening in the fence, the two of them small enough to fit through the arch cut into the metal wall without difficulty, while Maggie was a tight fit. She had to hug her mule's neck.

"Faster," Zoe screamed as the men shortened the distance between them.

The two women urged their mounts on, whipping the two animals furiously. The mule and burro heaved, thick layers of lather coating their necks and flanks, giving everything they had to run across the barren landscape towards the rocky cliff that loomed up from the desert floor.

Zoe's heart raced. A guttural growl escaped her lips. Panic seized her.

A staccato of machine gun quick shots rang out as the men opened fire. Zoe and Maggie zigzagged across each other's paths, trying to avoid the spree of bullets that tore divots in the sand all around them.

A black four-by-four bounced past them, the Signet of the US border agents on the door. The agents inside returned fire as the women continued to head for the red striated cliff and arroyo ahead of them. Above them, a remote controlled drone buzzed through the sky, circling the bandits.

Another burst of gunfire echoed over the desert. The drone burst into flames and careened out of the sky towards them.

"Look out," Zoe shouted, wheeling her burro sharply to the left. The drone crashed a few yards away from her. It splintered into a thousand little pieces.

"We'll hide in the canyon," Maggie hollered.

The mule broke into a trot, the burro still fighting to keep up, as they entered the steep walled canyon. Zoe thought poor O'Hara was going to collapse beneath her.

"We're almost there, buddy," she crooned, resting a hand on his neck.

Maggie checked over her shoulder. Zoe shot her a thumbs-up. She stopped, letting her mule catch its breath.

"I don't know about you," she huffed, "but I'm too old for this."

"Yeah, I have to admit," Zoe nodded, her chest heaving almost as hard as the burro's, "I'm with you there. I'm even starting to rethink this engagement thing."

Maggie smirked and rolled her eyes. She dismounted and gave the mule a pat.

"I think we better walk them for awhile," Maggie hissed. "The canyon narrows up here. I can see daylight ahead so it isn't a dead end."

"That's good," Zoe replied, almost falling off the burro.

The mule nuzzled Maggie.

"He's starting to like you," Zoe remarked casually. "I don't know why."

Maggie rolled her eyes and started walking up the canyon. They could still hear the firefight between the bandits and the border agents behind them. The sound of the gunfire bouncing off the canyon's wall's was panoramic.

"You know, I've been spit on and pulled over for driving while being coloured," Maggie continued. "I've been called a lot of things in my time, Zoe, including wagon-burner, spic, wetback, Pocahontas, but favourite has to be Mexican blackbird."

"I didn't know," Zoe gasped, shame setting fire to her cheeks. *Had Maggie heard her when she had called Maggie a Mexican blackbird when they first met?* Oh, the horror. She had meant it in jest.

"Yes, you did," Maggie growled, turning on her. "You're a racist, Zoe. Those kids back there. They weren't adorable. They're as starving as these two animals. That money I paid them is more than their whole family probably makes in two years. Those Mexicans that cleaned up after your horses are good hard working people. You could have at least taken the time to talk to them."

"Alright, alright, I hear you," Zoe griped, lifting her hands in surrender. Good grief, what had brought that on? "Perhaps I am a bit of a snob."

"A bit," Maggie replied tautly, unhooking the canteen's strap from around the saddle horn. She gave her mule a handful of water.

"Well you could let go of the 'bitch' routine some of the time," Zoe fumed, irritated. "I don't need this while we are in the middle of a war zone."

Zoe flipped open the cap on her canteen and took a swing of water. She then gave O'Hara some.

"I personally thought calling her a Mexican blackbird was a compliment," Zoe whispered to her burro. "Even under these horrid conditions, she looks ruddy marvellous. Look at me, broken nails, and hair like a brillo pad, split lips, and a bloody rash between my legs as wide as the Grand Canyon. Speaking of which, O'Hara, have you ever noticed that anything with 'Grand' in front of it is nasty."

Maggie snorted in amusement.

Zoe looked her compatriot in the eye and shrugged.

A stray bullet ricocheted over their heads. The mule and burro spooked, but settled down fast, more from exhaustion than anything else.

"How about this for a bandita's pose," Maggie suggested, wrapping an arm over the mule's neck, and making like she was a Bond girl holding a smoking gun.

Zoe grinned and attempted to sashay forward like she was a gangster carrying a machine gun, but doubled over in pain after two strides.

"Damn these saddle sores," she grumbled.

Maggie smothered a laugh.

"I'll see if I can find you some aloe in our travels," Maggie said, softening.

"Speaking of travels, do we have any idea where we are," Zoe whined.

"We're in America," Maggie grinned.

***

"You told us we were going home, yesterday," Sylvie spat, her temper flaring. "What's going on, Adonis?"

"Yeah, I'm done," Mary agreed. "My cowgirl-up has up and gone. I need a bath and a rib eye steak the size of North Dakota."

"Not Florida," Sylvie commented wryly.

"I think North Dakota is bigger," Mary muttered.

"Stop calling me Adonis," Percy quipped. "My name is Percy and I'm tired too."

"Well, Percy, I am seriously disappointed in you," Sylvie scolded her captor. "This is bull-hockey."

"And that's putting it nicely," Mary agreed.

"I see a dead man walking, don't you," Sylvie asked Mary.

Mary nodded.

"Yeah, well it's your boyfriend's fault. No one arrived at the drop with the money. Guess he doesn't love you after all," Percy yelled. "So, go turn that lemon into lemonade."

Percy stormed out of the room.

"We're in serious trouble, Sylvie," Mary croaked. "He's talking about fruit."

"I know," Sylvie agreed.

"Our only hope is for someone to find us," Mary sighed.

"About that," Sylvie leaned sideways, resting her head on Mary's shoulder as they sat leaning against the iron stove. "I have an idea, but you're not going to like it. I need you to play nice for the rest of the day."

"I am nice," Mary declared. "It's you that's a delinquent."

Sylvie guffawed. Percy wasn't the only one to notice the orange flags on the road and the plethora of horse tracks in the corral, not to mention the empty toilet paper roll in the outhouse.

"It isn't winning the race that counts, it's going the distance," Sylvie grinned, "and we are in the back stretch."

***

The sunset was a blaze of glory. It looked like a raging forest fire was sweeping through Heaven, and blasting open the Pearly Gates with a monstrous fireball.

Maggie watched as the flames died over head. It surprised her how fast night fell over the canyons. The stars were different from the ones she saw over the ranch, but just as pretty.

A coyote howled in the desert. A light wind carried its song over the magnificent landscape. She felt in touch peace for the first time in her life and it only took seventy plus years to find it.

Thanks to the kids and the pastor at Our Lady of Grace, they had a wonderful meal of cornbread and beans. A can opener and a Bic lighter had mysteriously appeared in a saddle bag. The fire in front of her was small, but delightful and chased away the chill. The burning wood smelled of sage.

The mule and burro lay close to the fire, content to be at rest. They had let them graze for an hour before the ladies settled down for the night.

Zoe mumbled in her sleep. She was restless and muttering incoherently, mixing up her husband's names. Maggie hoped it was just tiredness and not the dementia that had showed its ugly head last summer. The thought of Zoe wandering in the desert in the dead of night, alone and confused, was a terrifying thought.

Maggie looked at the lead rope hanging from the burro's halter, and went and unclipped it. She gently looped one end of the lead rope around Zoe's foot and the other around her wrist.

She sighed gently, searching the Heavens for a shooting star. They needed a lot more good luck to be able to get free of this predicament.

Eventually her eyes drooped. Her body ached all over. Soon, it would be over, she told herself, and then Zoe sat straight up in her sleep.

"Walter, for the love of God, why didn't you tell me you couldn't swim," Zoe scolded her deceased forth husband.

Chapter Twenty-Four

If it walks like a dog and barks like a dog, it is probably a dog.

Maggie and Zoe rode through the suburbs of the American border town; the houses were mostly adobe style ranch houses. A couple of gardeners cheered the two women riding the mule and burro through the neighbourhood on. Zoe and Maggie exchanged a travel weary look.

They had traversed several small creeks and one more river to get there, careful to skirt around the many ranches and herds of cattle they had come across. Whether the border patrol or the Mexican bandits were still after them was anyone's guess. They had purposefully ridden across the ninth fairway of a golf course, laughing in the faces of the irate golfers and grounds keepers who tried in vain to wave them off the course. It was a small bit of giddy fun in a day filled with endless vistas of sage brush and cactus.

A gas station attendant raced out of the pit stop grocery store combination with a bucket of water in each hand. Several people followed him out, pulling out their cell phones as they did so.

"Senioritas, senioritas, agua for your trusty steeds," the smiling attendant yelled, placing the buckets on the ground between the pumps and the road.

"Thank you," Maggie smiled, reining up beside him.

"It's my pleasure," the man grinned.

"Please, don't take any pictures," she begged the crowd.

The folks gathering around them smiled and nodded and continued to snap pictures and film their bizarre encounter.

"I don't suppose you have any sandwiches we can purchase," Zoe asked politely, "and some apples or carrots for our steeds. We finished off our provisions this morning."

"Si, si," the attendant said, rushing back into the store. He returned with a couple of chicken salad sandwiches and shopping bag full of apples and bottles of water.

Maggie tried to pay him with a hundred dollar bill, but he refused it. Zoe shrugged at the puzzled look on Maggie's face.

"Can you tell me where we are?" Maggie asked. "We didn't see any signs as we rode in."

"You are in Sonora," he responded.

"Arizona?"

"Si."

The crowd behind him was steadily increasing in size. Zoe noticed that everyone there was of Mexican descent. That's odd, she thought, but guessed it was because Sonora was a border town.

"I think we should leave, Mags," Zoe advised her friend.

"Are you sure I can't give you anything for your kindness," Maggie asked again.

"No, just a picture with me," he said, his smile getting even wider. "My wife won't believe me when I tell her I met you."

"Okay," Maggie agreed, even more confused.

The gas attendant posed beside Maggie and Cade, smiling into his phone as he snapped a picture. He then took a picture with Zoe and O'Hara.

Others ran forward to take a picture with the ladies and their mounts, when suddenly the 'whoop-whoop' of police sirens was heard speeding towards them.

"Let's go," Zoe cried in alarm, picking up the reins and kicking her burro forward.

"Down there, into the ditch," Maggie shouted back.

Maggie and Zoe rushed into the intersection. Several cars screeched to a halt. Two police cruisers screamed to a stop behind the cars. Four police officers jumped out, weapons drawn. The crowd at the gas station 'booed' the cops and ran interference for the ladies as the mule and burro skidded on the pavement as if it were ice.

Cade and O'Hara righted themselves once they got to the gravel shoulder.

The commotion in the street was deafening as people yelled at the police, forming a human chain to block them from following the ladies into the wide ditch.

The mule and burro jogged along the bottom of the dry ditch away from the escalating tensions between the law and their supporters. Ahead of them, the ditch veered left, towards the river they had followed into town. A man in priest's robes waved to them.

"Where did all these pastors come from," Maggie whispered fiercely to Zoe.

"Never question a man in a habit," Zoe smirked.

"Nuns wear habits, silly," Maggie groaned.

"Adelitas, here," the priest waved to them. "You must leave the river and ride along the parkway. When you see the farmer's market, turn right and follow that street until you see my church. I will give you and your mule and burro sanctuary."

"Why are you helping us," Maggie queried the young priest.

"Yes. And why are the police chasing us?" Zoe agreed.

"The border agents put the drone video up of you crossing the border and the firefight that ensued," the priest answered earnestly. "It's all over the news."

"Pesky drones," Maggie muttered.

"Maggie, we're wanted felons," Zoe gasped. "Isn't that marvellous?"

"Define 'marvellous'," Maggie hissed.

"You must hurry, my people can only hold the officers off for so long," the priest cried, waving them forward. "I will answer your questions later."

Maggie nodded and urged her mule forward. Zoe prodded her burro with a stick she picked up along the way, using it much like a riding crop. When Zoe looked back over her shoulder, the priest was running for his car. The priest reminded her of Gus Rodriquez. She found it funny that she should think of the ATF agent now.

Perhaps they should try phoning Gus from the church. It couldn't hurt to have an ATF agent intervene with the local authorities on their behalf.

***

Gus awoke to the sound of his cell phone ringing. Dee was already in the kitchen making breakfast. He grinned as he answered the call.

"McCaffrey, what's up?"

Gus listened to McCaffrey's recount of the two old ladies riding a mule and a burro over the Mexico/Arizona border. The locals were calling the ladies 'Soldaderas de la Madre Maria'. They had been spotted in Sonora. When the police tried to arrest them, they were forced back by a crowd of supporters. It was all over the news. McCaffrey thought it was hilarious.

Gus laughed and told him he'd be back next week. McCaffrey had teased him about helping his girlfriend start forest fires instead of putting them out and hung up.

He slipped on his jeans and wandered bare-chested into the kitchen where Dee was whipping four eggs in a bowl. Bacon sizzled in an iron fry pan.

"Morning, babe," he purred, wrapping his arms around his sweetheart. "That smells good."

"I promised Sam that we'd ride up to the mining town with him again. Jenny wants to do a trial run with Mike to make sure he can do it. With everything that is going on, I thought it would be a good idea for us to go."

"Works for me," he said, nuzzling Dee's neck.

"If you keep doing that, I'm going to burn the bacon," Dee scolded him.

Gus laughed.

"You wouldn't believe the crazy story my buddy just called to tell me about," Gus grinned. "Two old broads are on the America's Most Wanted list for crossing the border illegally on a mule and a donkey in a hail of bullets."

"Oh, my God, that is hilarious," Dee laughed.

"Yeah, the Mexican immigrants are calling them the Soldaderas de la Madre Maria which translates to Mother Mary's Soldiers. In the Mexican Revolution, there were lots of women in the army. Some even commanded their own units."

"Well, that's very progressive," Dee said, pouring the scrambled eggs into a pan.

"Not all of us are bandits, you know," he joked, kissing her on the neck before moving away to pour himself a cup of coffee.

"You know you could make yourself useful and put some bread in the toaster," Dee added.

Gus saluted her and did as he was ordered. Never anger a woman with a spatula in her hand was his motto.

Chapter Twenty-Five

Life is like a wild horse. You ride it or it rides you.

Sam and BJ unloaded the three already saddled horses and one very annoyed donkey from the stock trailer. The two dogs panted excitedly, tails wagging back and forth, one on each side of Jenny as she zipped up her jogging suit while doing some stretches.

A cold northeast wind blew down from the mountain, ruffling the horses' manes and tails and fluttering the bright ribbons in the donkey's tail.

Patch, Mary's dark bay and white blue-eyed paint stallion snorted as he lifted his nose to the wind. The seasoned stud travelled well, not batting an eye at the two prancing mares, their nostrils flared, flirting with the handsome male accompanying them. Once saddled, the stallion was calm and focused, ready to do whatever job was asked of him.

Dee pulled her truck and trailer in behind Sam's.

"Beautiful day isn't it," she called as she exited the truck.

"Too cold," Gus laughed from the other side of the truck.

"Wimp," Emma teased, buttoning up her jean jacket.

"It's not summer yet," Sam rumbled, handing Emma the reins to her pretty bay mare.

"Gus," Jenny squealed with delight, racing forward to embrace the rugged former marine.

"Jenny," Gus squealed back, hugging the little girl.

Everyone laughed.

"Good to see you, Em," Gus grinned, breaking away from Jenny and planting a brotherly kiss on Emma's cheek.

"Watch it, cowgirl, that's my man," Dee joked, unlocking the tailgate on her trailer. She then unloaded the two bay geldings.

"Hey, Dee," BJ blushed.

"Hey, cowboy," Dee replied. "That's a mighty fine stud you got there."

"I figured Mike might behave better if Patch was with him," BJ stammered, handing his sister the donkey's lead rope.

"Getting Mike to do what he's told is a mighty big ask," Dee agreed.

"You got that right," Jenny huffed, blowing a stray piece of hair out of her face.

"I figured me and Emma and you and Gus can ride on up ahead," Sam said, tightening up his red and white paint mare's cinch, and then swinging into the saddle. "BJ, you stay with your sister, Mike and the dogs. We won't be too far ahead if'n you need us."

227

BJ nodded as he stood by, one hand holding the reins, the other fastened around Junior's collar. The big pup's mum lay down in the gravel and waited patiently to be told what to do.

The squeak of leather and jangle of spurs and bits echoed through the air as Dee, Gus and Emma mounted their horses. The three bays danced side-by-side, playfully nipping at the neighbouring horse as the three jogged up the trail, Sam following up the rear.

Sam was happy to see his daughter-in-law smile. He hadn't seen her do that in days.

"BJ, I put a flare gun and a single flare in your saddle bag in case of a real emergency," Sam shouted, reining up for a minute. His mare reared and pinned back her ears. Sam moved her off his leg and jigged the reins to lower her head in submission. His mare always was a bit herd bound, not liking to go anywhere by herself.

"Okay, grandpa," BJ hollered back.

Sam nodded, spun his uppity reining horse around a couple of times to settle it down, and cantered to join up with the others.

Behind him, the donkey brayed sadly, calling after the horses.

In front of him, Dee's mustang reared and whirled to face the offensive sound.

Sam laughed himself silly. He'd forgotten the mustang hadn't met or heard the donkey before.

***

"Ready, sis," BJ asked his sister.

"Yeppers," Jenny giggled, finishing her stretches with a couple of deep knee bends and lunges.

"Away we go, girls," BJ told the dogs, letting go of Junior's collar.

The Saint Bernards barked and frolicked around Jenny and the donkey while BJ hauled himself up onto the paint stallion's back. The stallion waited patiently for the teen to settle in the saddle.

"Are you sure Mary won't mind you riding Patch," Jenny queried her brother, shortening the lead line.

"Are you sure your donkey will go up this trail without him," BJ retorted.

"Noooo," Jenny replied, tugging on the donkey's lead line.

"Didn't think so," BJ grinned as he started them off. "Gosh, I like this horse."

"You like every horse," Jenny said, jogging on the spot to show the donkey how it was done. "Come on, Mikey, we gotta keep up."

Mike let out another sad 'heehaw' and then lowered his head to sniff the trail. Jenny sighed in exasperation, tugged his head up, and dragged the donkey up the trail behind her brother on the paint stallion.

The wind whistled past them. Clouds scuttled across the sky. Despite the early spring, snow had fallen in the night in the mountains.

***

"You women are more trouble than you're worth," Benny raged, spittle flying in every direction.

"Come on, Benny, that's not nice," Percy wailed. "Leave them alone. It ain't their fault."

The punk haired rocker had been ranting all morning. Sylvie wanted to throw him over her knee and wail on his bottom like he deserved. Grown men shouldn't act like a toddler. She would have yelled, but Percy had duck taped hers and Mary's mouths shut when he heard the Bronco pull up behind the hotel.

Mary lay with her eyes closed, her jaw slack. Sylvie would have been worried except it was all part of the plan she had hatched last night. The party crasher was Mr. Screamer. The bozo just wouldn't leave.

"Wait, do you hear that?"

"Hear what?"

"Shhhh," Benny ordered Percy. "I hear voices. Keep them quiet."

Benny pulled a revolver out from under his jacket, waving it in the air to make a point.

Sylvie's eyes widened. She hadn't expected a gun.

"I'll deal with this," Benny growled, tucking the stubby revolver in his pocket as he headed for the door.

Sylvie could just make out the voices. One of them sounded like Sam's. His deep rancher's brogue was unmistakable. She thought she heard Emma's musical voice and a soft high pitched twitter that could only be Dee Gallant.

Oh, God, she prayed, *don't let that nutcase kill my friends.*

She glanced sideways. Mary's eyes flickered open. She had recognized the voices too and looked just as afraid as Sylvie was. They wanted to be rescued but not at the cost of a life.

"What're you doing up here, partner," she heard Sam thunder.

"Just exploring," Benny's voice hardened. "You got a problem with that old man?"

"Mind your manners, boy," another man replied harshly.

Was that Gus Rodriquez? What was he doing here? Of course, Sylvie reasoned, *he was either visiting Dee or perhaps joining the hunt to find them.*

Sylvie's heart soared. Gus would be armed.

"You're right, my apologies," the kidnapper said.

Yep, Gus was armed and showing his side holster off.

Even from this distance, Sylvie could hear the smirk in punk rocker's voice.

"This is a pretty cool place. Why the outhouses? It's pretty remote up here," the punk rocker continued.

"It's for the donkey race next weekend," Dee chirped.

"A donkey race? What's that," the kidnapper snorted in amusement.

"It's a fundraiser for the local elementary and high schools," Dee said. "Each entrant is paired with a donkey and they run a cross country course."

"And it's coming through here?"

Sylvie imagined Dee nodding agreement.

"You gonna be here long," Sam growled.

"Nope, just leaving," Benny said.

231

"My grandkids are on the back trail," Sam glowered. "I suggest you drive back that way."

Relief flooded through her as she heard Benny start up his Bronco and depart. She could see the stress leave Adonis' face as well.

She booted Mary and rolled her eyes, hoping the old cowgirl would read her mind: *close your eyes and look sick,* she wanted to shout. Mary let out a muffled groan and slumped sideways, her eyes closing.

"Hmmmm, hmmm, hmmm, hmmm," Sylvie mumbled beneath the sticky tape across her lips.

"Shut it," Percy wheezed, placing a finger to his mouth.

Sylvie rolled her eyes once again and nodded towards Mary's silent form.

"Is she alright," Percy whispered, poking Mary gently.

Outside, the sound of hoof beats receded into the distance.

"Hmmmm, hmmm, hmmm, hmmm," Sylvie tried again.

Percy scratched his head. He then reached down and yanked the tape off of Mary's mouth.

Sylvie's chest inflated with pride. Mary didn't make a sound.

"Is she sick," Percy asked her.

Sylvie shrugged helplessly.

"Don't you yell," he warned her, and then yanked the tape from her face.

"Ouch," Sylvie barked.

"What should I do," Percy asked worriedly. "I don't want her dying up here. I already gave her CPR once. I'm not sure I should do it again."

"So call 911," Sylvie exclaimed.

"I can't do that," he snorted, pacing the room.

***

"Miiiikkkkkeeee," Jenny whined, yanking as hard as she could on the lead line, but the donkey wouldn't budge. His one ear was set stubbornly backwards, his jaw set in a 'not going to do it anymore' pose.

BJ sat aboard the paint stallion rolling sideways in the saddle he was laughing so hard.

"It's not that funny," the little girl yelled at her brother.

"Look at it this way, you wanted to do a trial run to make sure Mike will go the distance, and now you have your answer," BJ chortled.

Jenny sat down in the middle of the road, her bottom bouncing off the ground. She glared upwards at the stubborn donkey.

"Tell you what, I'll go get grandpa. If Mike doesn't want to go any further, he doesn't have to. Grandpa can ride back down and drive up with the stock trailer to pick you up like he said he would. He won't mind."

Jenny rubbed the tears from her eyes and nodded dejectedly.

"Bulldozer, stay," BJ commanded the older Saint Bernard.

233

The dog rushed over and licked Jenny's face. She pushed the giant dog away.

"I'll see if I can find you another donkey to race with," BJ consoled his sister.

"It won't be the same without Mike," Jenny sniffed. "And my cowgirl grandmas aren't back anyway. What's the point?"

"I'll be back soon," BJ stammered, not knowing what else to say. He had been strictly forbidden to tell Jenny anything about the kidnapping.

BJ turned Patch and squeezed his legs together, loosening the reins as he did so. The stallion lifted his head and loped off in the direction of the mining town.

Jenny sat on the ground looking at the underside of Mike's long white chin whiskers. Dozer sat beside her. Junior barked, not knowing if she should follow BJ or stay with her mother and Jenny.

Mike's ear pricked up as the stallion disappeared around the bend in the trail. He honked and brayed.

"Patch is gone," Jenny moped, brushing the dirt from her behind as she stood up.

The donkey lunged forward, pulling the lead rope out of Jenny's hand.

"Mike, wait," Jenny yelled, chasing after the donkey as it galloped after its buddy, the dogs barking at its heels.

***

BJ trotted along the gravel road, his cheeks red from the punishing wind that whipped through the poplar and fir trees along the side of the trail. Checkers wore egg bar shoes so it was easy to see his grandfather's mare's hoof prints in the hard packed earth. The other horses' tracks weren't so deep.

All of a sudden, the paint skidded to a stop. He pricked his ears forward and nickered, the hair on the horse's neck standing on end.

"What is it, Patch," BJ asked worriedly. He hoped it wasn't a mountain lion. He had left Jenny with just the dogs to guard her.

Patch reared and pawed the earth. His shrill whinny almost shattered BJ's eardrums.

All at once the dogs galloped past him, barking furiously, the donkey hot on their heels, the lead rope trailing behind it.

"Dozer, Junior, you were supposed to stay with Jenny," BJ cried.

He reined the paint in a circle, trying to calm the jittery stallion, but the horse reared again, refusing to go back down the trail.

"BJ," he heard Jenny scream.

BJ leapt off the stallion, throwing the reins over the stud's head as he did so, and worked him in a circle, once again trying to get the horse to pay attention to him. Even the arrival of Mike didn't seem to make any difference.

Jenny jogged up the hill, one hand holding her side.

"Where are the dogs," she gasped.

"I don't know, I kind of have my hands full," BJ shouted.

"What's wrong with Patch," she yelled, skipping out of the way of the stallion's flying hooves.

"I don't know," BJ stammered, barely holding on to the frothing and bucking horse.

"I'll go find the dogs," his sister screamed, racing off in the direction of the historic mining town. "Maybe you should use that flare to call Grandpa."

***

Mary bolted upright as the two Saint Bernards barrelled into the room, knocking the young body builder flying.

"Dozers," Mary cheered with delight. "You found us."

The dogs leapt into her lap. They licked Mary's face until it looked like she had just stepped out of a shower.

"Good dogs," Sylvie cried, using the stove to haul herself to her feet. Her feet were free, but her hands were still tied.

Percy righted himself and struggled to pull the dogs off of Mary.

Sylvie spotted a cobweb strewn iron frying pan hanging on a hook on the far side of the stove. She grabbed it and smashed it into the back of Percy's head as Jenny raced through the hall into the hotel kitchen. The broad shouldered bodybuilder crashed to the floor.

"Mary! Sylvie!" Jenny screamed, slamming into the back of Junior. "You're supposed to be in Las Vegas."

"I wish," Sylvie grinned.

There was another loud crash as Mary's paint stallion, reins trailing behind him, burst into the small room.

"Patch," Mary yelled. "God bless you!"

"Whoa there, my friend, you're going to kill us all," Sylvie hollered, staggering forward. "Jenny, there's a paring knife on the table. Go get it and cut me loose."

Jenny skipped around the wild eyed stud crammed into the doorway, the two one hundred and forty pound dogs, the downed kidnapper, and Mary and Sylvie, to retrieve the black handled knife from a cutting board on a camp table in the corner.

"Patch," BJ moaned, struggling to get past the stallion.

"Mary! Sylvie!" he trembled, shocked at the sight of the two ladies, both hollow eyed and frail looking.

"Get those dogs off of Mary, BJ, and help her up," Sylvie commanded. "Oh, and tie that bozo up with that duct tape over there."

BJ nodded, his eyes wide with alarm, and ran over to Mary. He yanked the dogs off of her as Jenny made short work of the duct tape wrapped around Sylvie's wrists.

Mary stood up, her legs threatening to buckle, BJ holding onto one arm. Once she was stable, Jenny cut her bonds.

"I don't care how nice you tried to be to us," Mary quipped, planting a hard kick in Percy's side, "but you shouldn't be kidnapping helpless seniors."

Mary kicked him again.

Percy groaned at the impact.

"What," Mary snorted, looking into the amazed faces of the two kids and her friend. "You got to bonk him on the head!"

Sylvie snickered.

Patch pawed the floor boards.

"I love you guys so much," Mary gushed, hugging first BJ, and then Jenny, the dogs, and her stallion.

"Enough already," Sylvie chuckled. "Help me tie this guy up."

BJ raced to Sylvie's side. Sylvie grabbed a roll of duck tape and wrapped it around and around Percy's wrists as BJ held them tightly together and then the kidnapper's ankles.

"You got a rope, BJ," Sylvie grinned.

"On the saddle," BJ nodded, "but you can't get to it right now."

"Well back my big fella out of here and let's drag this so-and-so outside," Mary winked at the boy.

"Yes, ma'am," BJ replied excitedly.

The teen backed the old stallion out of the hotel, slipped the lariat off the saddle horn as Mary and Jenny watched. Sylvie motioned for BJ to give her the end of the rope.

"I'd prefer to hook him myself if you don't mind, ma'am," BJ nodded at Sylvie.

"Alright, cowboy, get 'er done," she drawled, standing aside.

"Can you hold onto Patch," BJ asked Mary, looking from the stallion to the dark, narrow hallway that he had to go back into.

"I'll do better than that," Mary grumbled. "Help me mount up."

BJ's eyes grew as round as an owl's, but he cupped his hands and Mary stepped into them. She hobbled up into the saddle, and picked up the reins, a wide grin spreading across her face. She signalled BJ to continue like Captain Picard on the Enterprise.

BJ shook out the lariat, strode past Sylvie, and into the hotel, a stern look on his boyish face.

"Let 'er rip," he yelled from inside the building.

"Back," Mary commanded, dragging the hapless kidnapper out of the building like a trussed up calf.

There was the sound of thundering hooves as Sam, Emma, Dee and Gus galloped out of the bush and into the yard.

"We saw your flare, BJ," Gus shouted.

"What in tarnation," Sam hollered, sitting deep in the saddle and coming to a sliding stop. He jumped out of the saddle and raced over to Sylvie.

The dogs barked furiously.

"Mary," Emma screamed with delight.

"Sylvie," Sam cried, wrapping his arms around her. "You're okay!"

"Don't crush me, Sam, I'm a little light on muscle right now," she grimaced, Sam's enthusiastic hug leaving her breathless.

"I see you got your man," Gus laughed, dismounting and walking over to stare down at the unconscious kidnapper.

"Another day and he would have let us go," Mary added. "He's a nice boy, just a little misguided."

Sylvie snorted back a remark about Mary kicking the bandit in the ribs, not once but twice.

Gus grinned as he pulled a set of handcuffs from his back pocket and looked over the duct tape job. He tried to fasten the handcuffs around the kidnapper's wrists, but the duck tape was too thick. He gave up and put the handcuffs back in his pocket.

Cole's Suburban rounded the bend. He stopped short of showering the group with gravel.

"Cole, what are you doing here," Emma beamed, dismounting.

"I was on the way here and saw the emergency flare. We collared the kidnapper, but he wouldn't give up his partner," Cole replied, taking in the scene before him. "He thought he could cut a deal. Guess that's not on the table now."

"Let me guess, the smart mouthed kid in the Bronco," Sam spat.

"How'd you know," Cole asked, puzzled.

"Met him," Sam harrumphed.

"And how did you know it was the boy in the Bronco," Emma queried her boyfriend, wrapping an arm around his waist.

"Tommy figured out it was his cellmate that came up with the idea," Cole grunted. "His son already had a rap sheet as long as my arm for petty theft and assault."

"I'm afraid Percy here may need to see a doctor," Sylvie shrugged. "He kind of connected with a frying pan on the way to the floor."

"Not to mention my boot," Mary added, the picture of innocence astride her heroic stallion.

"I helped too," Jenny chirped.

"You sure did," Sylvie laughed, planting a kiss on the top of the tow headed girl's head.

"And now you," Sylvie joked, chasing BJ around, her arms open for a hug.

The group all laughed, all except Percy, who was still out like a light.

Gus' cell phone rang shrilly. Gus pulled it out of his vest and glanced down at the display.

"It's the office," he told everyone.

"Hello," Gus said, picking up the call. "They're what?... And you're sure it's Maggie Carroll and Zoe Puddicombe asking for me?... I see. Okay, well, I'll be on the first plane out."

Everyone started asking questions at once, but Gus shushed them all.

"Look, tell the ladies that we caught the kidnappers. Sylvie and Mary are safe. I'm with them now," he told his supervisor and then hung up.

Sylvie, Mary, Sam and Dee, exchanged puzzled looks.

"Yeah, about that...," Cole stammered. "I had the weirdest call at the station."

"What's going on," Emma demanded, hands on her hips, her eyes blazing.

"It seems the two old ladies known as the Soldaderas de la Madre Maria are Maggie and Zoe. They're holed up in a catholic church in Sonora with the ransom money demanding sanctuary," Gus replied. "I have to go."

If it wasn't for the wind, Sylvie realized you could have heard the proverbial pin drop, until the donkey brayed and the mustang exploded.

Chapter Twenty-Six

Ole, ole, ole, ole, ... yes, it's hot, hot, hot!

"Father, I want you to take this for your troubles," Maggie commanded, handing Father Michael the lightest of the bags of loot. "It's just under a million dollars."

"I can't accept that," the priest answered, backing away.

"Yes, you can," Maggie smiled. "The government doesn't need it and you do."

"The people do," Zoe nodded in agreement.

"And it's mine to give away," Maggie argued. "We don't need it anymore."

"That's right, we don't," Zoe confirmed.

The priest shook his head in exasperation. He had come to know these women well in the past twenty-four hours. They wouldn't take 'no' for an answer so he reached for the bag.

"Father, let us in," the police chief yelled from outside the locked front door. "We'll break this door down if we have to."

"There sure are a lot of coppers out there," Zoe moaned, kneeling on a pew to look out the window. "And they're taking Cade and O'Hara away."

"How dare they," Maggie snarled.

The priest deposited the bag of cash Maggie gave him beneath his pulpit and pulled back the red skirting to hide it.

"Don't worry, they won't break down the door, this is a church. The people out there would riot. Come now, I have a way to get you out of here," Father Mike grinned.

Maggie and Zoe raced after the retreating priest to the rectory. Father Michael rolled up a beautiful carpet with a chorus of angels on it and yanked open a door in the floor.

"Like many of the old buildings and churches in the area, there are tunnels beneath it where people used to hide from the revolutionaries and the soldiers," the priest explained. "And my church is one of them."

"God bless you, Father," Zoe exclaimed.

Father Michael led the way down the stairs. The ladies followed carrying the last of the ransom money in the two gym bags. They crept through the dark tunnel, bent over as the tunnel ceiling was low and the walls narrow. Maggie felt instantly claustrophobic.

"Is that cars I'm hearing," Zoe asked. Her voice was sharp and piercing.

It heartened Maggie to know that Zoe was afraid as well. Maggie swore she could hear her heart beating. It was as loud as a kettle drum.

"We're here," Father Mike whispered, pushing up on a round metal drain cover.

"We won't get our heads chopped off by a passing car, will we," Zoe trembled.

"No, this drain opens up onto the parking lot across the street from the church," the priest assured them.

"You've been so kind, padre, once again, I can't thank you enough," Maggie said, gripping his hand in hers.

"Your courage and grace are enough," the priest returned, bowing his head. "And the money you gave me will help hundreds of people."

"Can you please make sure Cade and O'Hara don't end up in a meat market," Zoe cried. "I can't bear to think of them ending their lives that way."

"I will do my best," Father Mike agreed. "The mayor is part of my congregation."

Maggie felt some relief, but she and Zoe were still in a lot of trouble.

Maggie braced herself and stuck her head out of the hole. Several hundred people were gathered around the church including film crews, police, border agents, ATF agents, and the townsfolk of Sonora carrying signs that read: Liberar el Soldaderas de la Madre Maria!

"Who is the Soldaderas de la Madre Maria?" she asked the priest before climbing out of the hole.

"You are!"

"Huh?"

"You are legends. The money that you gave to the boys for the mule and the burro saved their family and the money you gave to our sister church has already fed many in need. You are legends, my friends," the priest gushed.

"We're legends, Mags," Zoe said, looking up from the bottom of the tunnel. "Can you imagine that?"

Maggie grinned. Who'd have thought?

"Vaya con dios," the priest murmured, crossing himself.

The area seemed to be clear. Maggie climbed out of the hole and held out her hand to help Zoe. Father Mike closed the round metal covering, disappearing back into the tunnel with a final wave.

The two women slipped behind a parked border patrol cruiser and glanced over the top. A little boy holding onto his mother's hand standing behind the police line saw them and waved. His mother looked to see what her son was waving at, saw them, and grinned. She whispered to the man standing next to her. He turned and smiled too. A murmur rippled through the crowd.

"Oh, no," Maggie spat. "We've been spotted."

Maggie inadvertently tugged on the cruiser's handle as she stood up. The cruiser's door popped open. Zoe's mouth dropped open in disbelief. Maggie shrugged.

"Soldaderas de la Madre Maria," the crowd shouted.

The news crews spun around, searching the crowd. The police chief yelled to his men. The crowd pushed back as the police and border patrol agents fought to secure the area.

Maggie and Zoe sneaked into the cruiser. Maggie searched under the driver's seat. She fingered a set of keys.

"For border agents, these guys aren't too swift," Maggie chuckled.

"Maybe they're part of Father Mike's congregation too, did you think of that?" Zoe murmured.

"Maybe," Maggie smiled as she flipped the key in the ignition.

"You know, we really don't need this money," Zoe said, looking at the crowd as it got more violent. "I don't want to see anyone get hurt."

"Me neither," Maggie agreed, a wicked gleam in her eye.

Zoe grinned and tugged the backpacks stuffed with cash into the front seat. She unzipped the zipper and pulled out a wad of hundred dollar bills.

"Are you thinking what I'm thinking," Zoe chortled. "No money, no crime?"

"Viva la Soldaderas de la Madre Maria," Maggie yelled, rolling down her window.

"Viva la Soldaderas de la Madre Maria," a woman yelled back, raising a fist in defiance.

Maggie inched the car forward into the crowd while Zoe threw stacks of bills out of the window. The crowd cheered, realized there were packets of hundred dollar bills in the street and went wild. The police and border agents didn't stand a chance as they were swarmed by Maggie and Zoe's supporters.

Maggie laughed. This was the best day of her life. If she had to spend the rest of her time on earth in jail, then she would happily do so. Sylvie and Mary were safe. Sam would look after Desert Storm. What more could she ask?

Chapter Twenty-Seven

It ain't over until the fat lady sings.

Tommy watched Bruce Park's son join his father on the walk of shame between the rows of screaming cons on this cell block. The fat man, sporting a nasty black eye, and a bruise across the right side of his face, and his newly shorn son, tucked their chins into their chests. The young man's bravado had been replaced with abject fear.

"Dead men walking," screamed some inmates.

"Fresh meat," yelled others.

The Park family was being sent to a different cell block for their own protection. His former cellmate wasn't going to get out in five years anymore. He would die in prison. It didn't matter to Tommy. He would get his revenge; he had all the time in the world.

The cartel was mollified when he told them where to find Marco. In general, Tommy was not just respected but well liked, especially amongst the Spanish population. Everyone knew the Soldaderas de la Madre Maria were his ladies. Zoe had cancelled their engagement. He was okay with that. He realized throughout the ordeal that he loved the hot tempered Maggie a little more than the ditzy chic.

Tommy automatically backed up to the back of his cell when a guard brought in his new cellmate.

"Buenos dias, amigo," Tommy grinned.

The good looking blond boy in front of him paled, his lower lip trembling. The guard unfastened the handcuffs around his wrists and nodded to Tommy before he closed the steel door shut behind him.

"You are a very lucky man, Percy James," Tommy whispered into the young man's ear. "You owe my lady friends and their friends a very large debt of gratitude. For some reason, the ladies like you. They made me promise to be nice. This is me being nice. How do you like me so far?"

***

Sweat dripped down Jenny's face as she passed her school mates, Sarah and Jenna, their donkeys shorter legged than her own. She didn't have time to smile or revel in her accomplishments. There were still four more competitors in her age group ahead of her.

She didn't realize how hard it was going to be to run uphill until a few days ago when she chased after Mike. Next year, she'd train on the trails instead of in the ranch yard.

Bulldozer and Junior ran beside her, tongues lolling. She wasn't going to let them run with her, but the dogs had other ideas.

"Still doing okay, sis," BJ asked from the back of his buckskin gelding as he jogged to keep up with her.

She nodded, running past the last water stop before the steep climb to the top of the hill and the finish line.

"Sweeetttt," he grinned.

Behind her, she heard a loud honking bray as someone's donkey bolted away from their handler. BJ galloped off to chase down the loose donkey.

Jenny's side was hurting. A stitch ripped through her right side beneath the rib cage. She squirted water from the water bottle in her hand into her mouth and kept going, determined to win.

She was forced to break down to a walk, but at least the two boys and one girl ahead of her now were doing the same thing. They had to look out for their four legged racing buddies too.

The donkey at her side nuzzled her. She poured a little water into her hand and he snuffled it down. She then gave a little water to the two dogs at her side. They lapped it up gratefully.

"Almost there," she mumbled, placing the cap back on the water bottle. "You're the man!"

Jenny inhaled a deep breath of cold mountain air. It was a glorious day for a donkey race. The sky was bright blue. The sun was warm, but not too hot.

Jenny reached down deep and despite her screaming calf muscles broke into a jog. The dogs and donkey matched her pace.

"Go Jenny," she heard her mother shout from the top of the hill.

Jenny grinned. She was there! She could see the red flags marking the finish line.

"Go O'Hara," her cowgirl grandmas screamed in unison. "Go, Jenny!"

Jenny grinned briefly. She was so glad the ladies were there to watch her race and grateful to Zoe for letting her burro, O'Hara, be her racing partner. Cade, Maggie's mule, and O'Hara, had settled right in with Patch and Mike when they arrived off the plane from Arizona.

The dogs were the true heroes though, their love for their family boundless. Maggie and Zoe were pretty amazing too. The Governor of Arizona agreed: he pardoned them after a call from the Mayor of Sonora, plus Jenny had overheard Gus and her grandfather saying the Governor would never win another election if he prosecuted the Soldaderas de la Madre Maria.

"Come on, O'Hara, we got this," the little girl gasped, pushing herself on. Slowly she overtook the racers ahead of her.

She heard hoof beats beside her, but didn't dare turn to look.

"Run, Jenny, run," BJ shouted.

"Go, go, go," Ranger Dee shouted from the back of her Quarter horse.

"You got this, kid," Gus Rodriquez yelled as he ran up beside her, matching her pace. She thought Gus looked cute in ladies pink gym shorts and a purple t-shirt, the same colours that Jenny wore as her race colours.

She looked up and saw her grandfather, his arm around Sylvie O'Hara, her mother and Sheriff Trane holding hands, and Maggie Carroll and Zoe Puddicombe, waving to her from the finish line. Each one of them wore t-shirts or sweaters in her colours, and black cowboy hats.

It was the perfect day for a donkey race.

The End... okay, not quite

I hope you enjoyed *Bandits, Broads & Dirty Dawgs*. Please consider leaving a review on *Amazon*, Goodreads , Bookbub or give the book a shout out on your Facebook or Twitter feeds.

If you haven't read it yet, check out the book that started it all: *The Silver Spurs Home for Aging Cowgirls*.
Thanks to fan requests, **the series continues with *Who Killed Cade*.**

Don't forget the **black comedy cozy mystery series with a wayward pig, a Jersey cow, and a whack of courageous dogs:** *Gumboots, Gumshoes & Murder*. It is a laugh out loud murder mystery series for those who enjoy *Miss Marple, Murder She Wrote, Glock Grannies, and Carl Hiaasen.*

Looking for a **great family story with horses**, take a boo at The Holiday Series including: *One Frosty Christmas, The Great Pumpkin Ride, A Filly Called Easter, Independence and Valentino.*

Peace and wellness.

Who Killed Cade-

A Preview

Who Killed Cade - Prelude

To ride a horse is to ride the wind.

The bandy-legged old man stood at the rail wearing a nondescript brown oilskin raincoat, a stained Tilley hat cocked jauntily to one side, a long silver ponytail poking out from beneath it, his icy blue eyes fixed upon the gangly dappled grey stud colt prancing by on its way to the gate. The jockey, dressed in burgundy and silver, allowed the colt named Steam Train to skip sideways towards the rail. The jockey caught the old man's eye briefly and then looked away. There was an imperceptible nod, a slight dip of the chin as the colt kicked out at the side walker's horse. The old man grinned crookedly.

Steam Train was the favourite to win, the odds only two to one, but if he placed, the odds were five to three.

Sean Finnegan, the owner and trainer of Steam Train, and his silver-blond faded trophy wife, Lacy, matched the pace of the horse along the rail. The couple strode by him, the horse's owner not even muttering an apology as he jostled the grey-haired spectator. Lacy's brown eyes glittered with mirth, her lips puckering into what she thought of as a come-hither smirk as her finger's casually brushed against the old man's before she disappeared into the crowd, her colourful rose patterned umbrella marking her progress. The pony-tailed senior would have laughed, but there was an ironic sadness to the situation that wasn't lost upon him.

Behind Steam Train walked the long shot at fifty to one. The chestnut filly's name, One Flashy Dame, didn't suit her. The filly wasn't flashy at all. She had a pencil thin neck, spindly legs, thin frame and an almost apologetic demeanour, despite being a descendant of the great Secretariat. The filly was entered into the Cup at the last minute after two scratches two days earlier. One Flashy Dame was owned by a singularly happy old lady with more money than sense.

One Flashy Dame had only run two races, floundering at the back of the pack so her true abilities were yet to be discovered. The filly had steadfastly refused the jockey's whip and urgings to run faster. She had remained like that until yesterday when her regular jockey was thrown during a training ride on another horse and broke his collar bone. A young girl with coal black hair and an infectious grin agreed to ride the filly for her elderly aunt after just receiving her jockey's license. This was going to be her first professional ride.

The old man had strolled through the stables the day before with an air of confidence, looking every bit the seasoned stock agent. No one questioned him. He stopped outside of One Flashy Dame's stall to congratulate the girl and to wish her good luck.

"Thank you," the girl grinned. "Me and Flash are going to crush it tomorrow, you wait and see. Flash doesn't like men, especially that lame brain who's been riding her."

"Is that so," the man smiled in return, turning on the charm. His blue eyes sparkled merrily as he held out his palm for the filly to sniff. 'Flash' as the girl called the filly sniffed his palm and then nuzzled his cheek, licking her lips in the process.

"Oooh, make a liar out of me, eh, girl," the jockey stuttered, her British accent kicking in.

"She's got good taste, is all," the balding horseman whispered, lovingly stroking the filly's soft velvet nose. "I rode a mare like her years ago. She'd have taken me all the way to the top if I hadn't had a falling out with the owner."

"Really," the girl said, shooting him a questioning look.

"That accent of yours, it's from Birmingham isn't it," he queried.

"It is. How did you know?" the girl grinned.

"I worked with a couple of lads from there. When I was your age all I could think of was racing," the soft-spoken horseman said, his eyes taking on a faraway look. "I was too tall for here and went to Ireland first and then England.

I was thin as a reed then and willing to get on anything with four legs. Like you, it was my first professional ride. The mare's name was Star Crossed. It did her justice. She was a rangy mean tempered cow, tossed anyone foolish enough to throw a leg over her, but oh that mare could jump. It took me awhile, but finally Star Crossed and I came to an understanding."

"You were a steeplechase jockey," the girl gushed, suitably impressed.

"Aye, one of the best until I got blackballed by Star Crossed's pompous owner," the retired steeplechaser growled. "I banged about for awhile at various training stables, but the good ones wouldn't hire me, so I came home."

The tiny jockey patted his shoulder sympathetically.

"Because Flash obviously likes you and you're one of us," the girl whispered fiercely, carefully glancing around to make sure no one was within ear shot, "I'll tell you a secret."

"I don't know, luv, I don't keep secrets well," the old man replied with a shake of his head.

"Wager big on my girl tomorrow," the jockey murmured. "The weather's supposed to turn. Flash loves to run in the rain. She can take that grey in the mud any day. Also, that no talent sod who was riding her used the whip too much and she doesn't respond to that, only the voice. You got to sing to her. The faster the song, the faster she runs."

The retired jockey slapped his leg and laughed raucously. Women, they were all the same. You just needed to figure out what inspired them to get them into the winner's circle.

"I'll do that missy," he crooned to the inexperienced jockey. "You and Flash make a good team."

"Thank you," the girl beamed. "Oye, what's your name? I'll watch for you in the stands."

"O'Hara," the old man answered with a mischievous grin. "Just call me O'Hara."

"It was nice to meet you Mister O'Hara," the jockey finished, waving a goodbye to the funny balding retired jockey.

"You too, sweetie," he laughed heartily. "And you as well Flash."

The filly in the stall snorted and nuzzled him once more.

Why not, he thought to himself as he sauntered back towards the exercise yard where Steam Train's jockey was climbing aboard the grey colt, *no reason not to bet on the rookie jockey and sleepy-eyed filly. Maybe lightning would strike twice. Wouldn't that be a hoot?*

***

That was yesterday. This was today. The girl was right. The track before him was a muddy mess. The down pour that started around midnight had receded into a light drizzle, but the damage was done.

He left the rail and strode quickly through the crowd up to the long line of ticket booths inside the main building. He approached the wicket that he had been using to place his bets all day and put ten thousand cash down on One Flashy Dame to win.

"Criminy, you aren't serious," the boy at the ticket booth asked. The kid looked sixteen, not twenty-one, the peach fuzz on his chin barely passing for a beard. "You're going to blow everything you won today."

"What can I say, I love underdogs and redheads," he chortled, "and not necessarily in that order."

"Your loss," peach fuzz shrugged, handing the old man the ticket.

The retired jockey had already called his bookie to place his main bet: twenty-five thousand on Steam Train to place. His bookie had thought he was as daft as the kid did, but the girl had inspired him. Steam Train to place was a given. One Flashy Dame had a chance if the cocky young jockey was right.

The starting horn bellowed. The horses were off. O'Hara hurried back down to the gate, jostling through the crowd of raincoat clad betters until he was leaning over the rail beside the finish line.

Steam Train barrelled around the track, in the lead from the start. It was clear the grey colt was a contender for the Kentucky Derby if he continued to run like he did now. The jockey couldn't hold him back. Had O'Hara just blown thirty-five thousand?

One Flashy Dame and the cute little gal atop of her were at the back of the pack, eating mud, but halfway around the oval, the chestnut filly started to gain ground. A ray of sun peeked out from between the scuttling clouds, the light drizzle that had been falling suddenly subsiding.

Waves of fog drifted along the ground making it look as if the galloping horses were painted metal pieces on a game board, their legs completely cut off by the swirling grey mist.

The retired jockey willed the filly on, revelling in the girl's expert handling of the thoroughbred. He wondered what song she was singing to the surging horse.

An opening appeared between two bays and the chestnut ploughed through it.

"And it's Locomotion in second, Everlasting Glow in third, three strides behind Steam Train. Wait! Holy cow, it's One Flashy Dame on the outside moving fast. Look at that filly run," the announcer cried.

"Come on, Flash," the old man yelled, pounding the rail with a fist, his eyes alight, his cheeks reddening as if he too was astride the filly as it barrelled past Everlasting Glow and Locomotion.

"It's Steam Train and One Flashy Dame heading for the finish line," the announcer screamed as the crowd in the stands went wild.

"It's One Flashy Dame in the lead," the announcer hollered excitedly. "Now its Steam Train by a nose, but here comes One Flashy Dame on the outside. It's One Flashy Dame! It's One Flashy Dame! The long shot, One Flashy Dame, with rookie jockey Sadie Nesbitt on board has just won the Cup. What an upset!"

The retired steeplechase jockey hooted encouragement as the chestnut filly cantered a victory lap past the stands, soupy mud flying in every direction, the raven-haired jockey standing in the stirrups looking more like a mud wrestler than a rider, her green and gold jockey silks barely recognizable, and one hand raised in the air in triumph.

Sadie noticed the old man leaning against the rail and shot him a thumbs-up sign. He tipped his hat to her in a silent salute.

Behind One Flashy Dame cantered the former favourite, Steam Train. The jockey shook his head in mock consternation as he rode the mud splattered grey stud colt past some very angry betters.

O'Hara followed the crowd to the winner's circle, unable to suppress his joy. One Flashy Dame and her diminutive jockey together had just won him a half million bucks.

He was delighted to see the filly's owner, aided by a racetrack employee, hobble into the winner's circle to receive an armful of red roses from the racetrack manager. The old woman reminded him of Queen Elizabeth so regal was her stance and wave to the crowd of onlookers, the bouquet of roses almost as tall as she was.

"You idiot," Sean Finnegan shouted at his jockey. "How the Hell could you lose to that fleabag? And to a rookie jockey?"

The crowd booed loudly as the grey colt spooked sideways away from the furious trainer.

"Just wasn't our day, boss," the old man heard the jockey say. "Train's not a mudder."

One of the course administrators raced to the scene, hauling Finnegan to one side to caution him. Lacy Finnegan, ever the lady, took a moment to speak a few words of encouragement to Sadie and her over-the-moon happy auntie, ignoring the furious glances of her husband.

O'Hara would have laughed, but the smile was wiped from his face when the jockey aboard Steam Train shot him a pointed look.

Really, the old man grimaced. *You think you're going to get paid when One Flashy Dame clearly won the race by sheer talent?*

The old man whistled happily as he walked up to his favourite ticket window.

The kid behind the window shot him a high-five through the Plexiglas.

"Man, you sure called it. I got to wait for the manager for this though," peach fuzz grinned. "The track manager will want a picture with you and your winnings cheque, I'm sure."

"No pictures," the pony tailed punter responded, his visage clouding over.

"Okay, but I still need your name for the cheque," the kid wheedled.

"Make it out to… Cade O'Hara," the old man grinned, his trepidation fading. "That's C.A.D.E. Cade with a 'C', and O. Apostrophe. H. A. R. A. O'Hara."

"I can spell, you know," peach fuzz grumbled.

Who Killed Cade - Chapter One

Life without you would be a pointless pencil.

"I think it's going to be a hot one today," the pretty forest ranger crooned in Gus' ear, snuggling up beside him as he finished washing the last of the breakfast dishes.

They had made a deal: the cook didn't have to clean. Dee's breakfast of scrambled eggs, sausages, bacon, fried ham and flapjacks would last him until supper time. It was only fair he clean-up after the class five hurricane named Gallant swept through the kitchen. Even then, Gus figured he got the better end of the deal.

"Let's ride up to the lake before it gets too hot," Gus suggested, drying his hands on a dish towel.

He swivelled around, reaching out to the woman curled around him like a python and swept a lock of dark hair from her upturned face.

"And what kind of trouble should we get into at the lake," she grinned, her brown eyes sparkling with mischief. "Something naughty, I hope."

"I can think of a few things," the handsome ATF agent whispered into her luscious hair, the soft scent of her coconut shampoo tickling his nostrils.

"I'll go saddle the horses," the ranger laughed, pulling away.

"You do that," he grinned.

Dee swatted him playfully on the behind before exiting the house.

Gus watched his girlfriend sashay across the yard towards the barn, her arthritic Border collie walking slowly behind her. The dog didn't come on trail rides anymore, too crippled with age to endure the miles of rough terrain. They had almost adopted one of the Montana's Saint Bernard puppies last year, but it wouldn't have been fair to the collie.

Sometimes, Gus's love for the sensuous forest ranger overwhelmed him... like now, his pulse was beating so fast, he thought his heart was going to explode out of his chest like the creature in the movie 'Alien'. When he wasn't with Dee, he longed for her. Gus wanted to be with her every moment of every day, now and forever, protecting her, loving her. He wanted to know that when he came home, she would be there.

Gus sighed. He had never had a real home, only one foster home after the other growing up until he joined the marines, but now this small acreage in the middle of nowhere felt like the place he belonged.

He had seven days left to put his plan into motion. Fingers crossed; it would go without a hitch.

Outside the house, Dee grabbed a couple of halters and walked across the pasture towards the bay mustang and Quarter horse grazing in the field. The horses whinnied as they greeted her.

The mountains in the distance looked like a watercolor painting, the multilayered shades of green, grey and brown muted by the early morning heat haze. The sky was pale blue. Traces of long white clouds hovered above the mountain tops. The fields in the valley were mostly brown, the last of the season's hay already cut and drying in the sun.

The hardened Afghanistan vet's strong jaw line and brown eyes softened as he observed the scene with childlike wonder.

Gus pulled his cell phone out of his back pocket and dialled his sister. She was an early riser.

"Yo, bro," his sister laughed, picking up the call on the second ring. "I'm just heading down to breakfast. Good timing. What's up?"

"I need your help," Gus chuckled, imagining the redheaded minister pushing the glasses up her nose as she talked, a habit she had since childhood.

"Do I need to wear my vestments?" asked the smooth silky voice.

"No," he chuckled. "I'm planning on asking Dee to marry me and I want it to be special."

"Ahh, now even I'm blushing," his sister replied.

"You know how I told you she's always rescuing wounded animals," Gus grinned. "Well, I had this idea to send her out looking for a wounded owl or eagle or something like that, but instead of finding the bird, she'd find me with a ring and a bunch of flowers."

There was a pause at the end of the line followed by a hearty laugh.

"Bro, I never knew you were such a romantic," was the startled reply. "I'm in. I can't wait to meet the woman who has turned my brother into mush. I would suggest that 'a bunch of flowers' bears thinking about."

"Okay, okay, maybe roses. Heck, I don't know if she even likes them," Gus said, exasperated. Leave it to his sister to want to know every detail. She was always like that.

"Chill, man, I just want to help. Once she finds you instead of a bird of prey, not that you don't fit into that category, exactly what are you going to say?"

"I dunno, maybe say something like 'life without you is like a pointless pencil, and now it's not pointless anymore," Gus answered, not having given that part much thought.

"Yeah, maybe work on that a little," the pastor laughed. "I suggest you stay with the basics, you know, a stupidly expensive gigantic diamond ring followed by a 'will you marry me?'"

"Dee's not the type to want a gigantic ring. It would make it hard to bridle a horse, might poke an eye out, but I hear you, sis. When can you be here?"

"In a few days," she replied. "The retreat is over tomorrow. I have an interview with the archbishop today about a posting he can't fill, plus I've got a eulogy to perform for a couple of biker friends and then I'm all yours."

"Sounds good. Take care and I'll see you soon," he grinned.

"Will do."

Gus ended the call. The one good thing that came out of his scattered upbringing was his sister. Once they met, two kids alone in the foster system, they vowed never to leave each other. They had kept that vow, but he hadn't seen her in three years. Gus couldn't wait for Terri and Dee to meet.

The rest was pure planning. How hard could it be? Right? Emma and Sam Montana were his next recruits. They could help him finalize his engagement plans. Funny, him asking Emma for help. He had promised Cleve, Emma's husband that he would look after her if Cleve didn't make it back from Afghanistan. Gus had been attracted to his best friend's widow at first and wanted to fulfill his promise to her husband, but Emma was already smitten. Sheriff Cole Trane was the focus of her desire.

The moment Gus laid eyes on the ranger riding up the canyon, a wanted felon on her horse, he was hooked. She was something out of a Conan the Barbarian novel, both beautiful and wild. Life without Dee was too horrible to contemplate.

"I'm not saddling your horse for you," Dee yelled from the barn breaking into his reverie.

"Coming," Gus hollered in return, stuffing his cell phone back in his rear pocket.

Life was good, he mused as he sauntered out of the house towards his soon-to-be fiancée, the screen door banging shut behind him. *Yep, life was good indeed and he was pretty sure Dee would say 'yes'.*

***

"I think we should all go for a ride after breakfast," Mary said, using her fork as a pointer stick. "The horses could use an outing and so could we."

"Oh, I don't know," Zoe replied diffidently, pushing an unruly strand of grey hair out of her face. "I need to go into town and get a trim."

"Yes, you look like Harry Potter," Sylvie joked.

"I do not," Zoe grumbled. "My hair isn't even black anymore. Wait, do you think I should dye it?"

"I'm just pulling your leg," Sylvie laughed.

"You can get your hair done any time," Mary argued.

"Mary's right, we should go for a ride," Sylvie agreed. "It will be too hot later on to do anything but nap or preen ourselves, preferably in some place with air conditioning."

Sylvie's compatriot, Mary Adams, a Dolly Parton look-alike, glanced her way. The pair exchanged a grin. Laugh lines creased the corners of Mary's blue eyes.

Sylvie smirked as she looked around the table at the fellow residents of The Silver Spurs Home for Aging Cowgirls. After five years in a wheelchair thanks to a massive stroke, the move to the Montana ranch, the subsequent death of her cheating husband, the disappearance of his body, and her kidnapping by two bumbling bandits, a peaceful morning ride was just the ticket to kick off the day.

Zoe rolled her brown eyes.

Ever since Zoe and Maggie had ventured into Mexico to retrieve three million dollars of ransom money to free her and Mary from the kidnappers, Zoe's ten minutes of fame on national TV had made Zoe more than a little overbearing. Zoe's ego had swelled to monstrous proportions.

"What do you think, Butch," Zoe queried the black-haired sultry woman of Spanish Cherokee Irish origins sitting to the left of her.

"Don't call me that," Maggie snapped. "And stop insisting I call you Sundance. It's annoying."

Maggie Carroll was still beautiful at seventy-three years-old, but she had soured since she had stopped visiting the notorious smuggler Tommy Cortez in prison. Not that she'd been a happy person to begin with, Sylvie mused, but Maggie's depression was sucking the life out of her and everyone else at the table.

Zoe and Maggie had been bitter rivals for a time. Now, they did everything together, albeit with a feline cattiness that would make a preacher blush. They had terrorized the blackjack dealers in Vegas after the kidnapping fiasco. Mary and Sylvie had joined them once the doctors had given them the okay. Those were good times. It felt like eons ago.

"I suppose Storm could use an adventure," Maggie mumbled into her coffee cup. "He has been a bit uppity lately."

"Mags, Storm is always uppity," Sylvie chortled.

"I guess Zippo could use some down time too," Zoe finally agreed. "BJ's done a marvelous job with him, but a day out of the ring would do him good."

'It's settled then," Mary laughed lightly, clapping her hands together. "We'll take the stallions out."

"What's settled," Sam Montana asked, striding into the room. He made a beeline for the coffee pot, his cowboy boots clumping across the hardwood floors, his sweat stained Stetson tipped back on his head, his white moustache twitching as he eyed the ladies suspiciously.

Sylvie felt her pulse quicken. Sam Montana cut a striking figure with his tanned face, hazel eyes, and salt and pepper hair. He gazed down upon her, his head tilting slightly sideways. The look he gave her made her heart flutter.

Part of Sylvie wished desperately that they could find Cade's body and get it over with. She had confessed to killing him, but then Cade up and walked right out of the outhouse where she had placed him. Cade always was contrary though, so it wasn't a complete surprise.

Still, a body would be helpful. If Zoe and Maggie could have conjugal visits with a felon, then surely Sylvie could arrange for conjugal visits with Sam. Sam was such a God-fearing man; the only way their unspoken love would ever be shared was if Cade turned up, dead or alive.

"We're going for a trail ride," Sylvie grinned, eyes fixed upon Sam. "The studs need a little time in the saddle."

"They do, do they?" Sam chuckled.

"They aren't the only ones," Mary muttered into her teacup.

Sam and Sylvie smothered a laugh.

"Do you think Emma will be home soon," Zoe queried. "Maybe she'd like to come with us?"

"Nice thought, but don't count on her," Sam said, refilling his coffee mug. "She's picking up groceries and has some other errands to run after she drops the kids off at their friends' houses."

"Well, then we may as well run upstairs and change into our breeches," Maggie declared, pushing away from the table.

"Indeed," Zoe agreed, daintily dabbing her mouth with a napkin.

"While you two get all dolled up for your stallions, Sylvie and I will clear the table," Mary chastised the pair.

"You don't have to," Sam grumbled. "Emma will clean the kitchen when she gets back. That's what you're paying us for."

"Sam Montana, I think we are more than capable of putting our own dirty dishes into the dishwasher and wiping down the kitchen counters for Emma," Sylvie quipped.

"Yes, ma'am," Sam stammered, raising his hands into the air in supplication.

"You two need to get a room and get it over with," Mary laughed, wagging a finger at Sylvie and Sam. "And don't go looking at me like that, Sam. I've known you way too long. It's about time you got off that high horse of yours."

Sam guffawed, blushing from head to toe. Sylvie fought the urge to throw herself across the kitchen table at him. He looked so darn adorable.

Maggie glowered. Zoe laughed delightedly, having given up long ago on convincing Sam to be husband number seven.

"I'll go water the stallions before you go," Sam harrumphed, performing a quick about face and racing out of the room as Maggie and Zoe marched out of the kitchen behind him.

"Well, that's one way to clear a room," Sylvie joked to Mary.

She and Mary burst out laughing.

Other Books by Laura Hesse

<u>The Holiday Series (family adventure):</u>
One Frosty Christmas, The Great Pumpkin Ride, A Filly Called Easter, Independence and Valentino

<u>Paranormal Thriller:</u>
The Thin Line of Reason

<u>The Gumboot & Gumshoe Series:</u>
Book One: *Gumboots, Gumshoes & Murder*
Book Two: *The Dastardly Mr. Deeds*
Book Three: *Murder Most Fowl*
Book Four: *Gertrude & The Sorcerer's Gold*
Book Five: *Chasing Santa*

<u>The Silver Spurs Series:</u>
The Silver Spurs Home for Aging Cowgirls
Bandits, Broads, & Dirty Dawgs
Who Killed Cade

<u>Comedy & Adventure:</u>
Peter Pan Wears Steel Toes

If you want to find out more about Laura Hesse or hear about her upcoming releases, then visit:
<u>www.RunningLProductions.com</u>

Epilogue

A heartfelt thank-you goes out to fans that have left reviews on Amazon, Goodreads, and Facebook or reached out by email via my website at www.RunningLProductions.com. Because of you, my readers, I added another two books to *The Gumboot & Gumshoe Series* and added a third book to *The Silver Spur Series - Who Killed Cade*.

The seeds were sewn for *Who Killed Cade* in *Bandits, Broads, & Dirty Dawgs*. Did you spot them? Don't worry if you didn't, the next book will be a whole lot of fun.

About the Author

Laura lives on Vancouver Island with a rescue dog and two old cats. She grew up a back stage brat in Music Hall Theatre and credits her mother with her love of song and theatre. She loves to sing at local jams when she can.

All of Laura's horses have passed over the rainbow bridge, but they will forever live on in the pages of her books.

www.ingramcontent.com/pod-product-compliance
Lightning Source LLC
Chambersburg PA
CBHW071127260626
47162CB00003B/697